MARYANN LANDERS

ALASKAN WOMEN OF CALIBER SERIES

MARYANN LANDERS

Book Cover Design: Pro_ebookcovers, Fiverr

Editors: Jessica Martinez Copywriting and Editing Services and Kameo Monson Editing Services

❀ Created with Vellum

This is for Lou.

Thank you for allowing God's transformation in your Alaskan Calibration so that you would yield a Godly legacy for your family! You are loved!

PREFACE

This story was based on actual events except of course when they didn't happen and the people didn't exist. I muddled the time frame and changed elements for dramatic purposes.

There also weren't any real or imagined puppies or bears harmed in the writing of this novel. Nor were any teenage children of the author starving while she was writing (although they may have claimed to be). The unnamed teens may or may not of stolen or hidden snacks real or imagined from the pantry or freezer.

PROLOGUE

MICHIGAN 1963

DON'T MUDDLE UP.

I spoke the words firmly to myself, not wanting to mess up this chance at a date. I curved my legs against the car door and stole a brief glance over at Roy. The masculine smell of Old Spice in this macho-man's car mesmerized my senses, setting Roy apart from any guy I'd noticed so far. Holding back a whoop of elation at the thrill of landing shotgun in Roy Wendel's blue Pontiac convertible, I braced my core with my clammy arms. Where would this adventure take us on a sultry summer night?

It was my first date—a double with my brother Norman and his girlfriend. It was Norm's birthday, and earlier in the evening, he'd invited Roy, a friend from work, to the house and asked him to grab some drinks along the way. We'd sat around the house talking until Roy suggested we take the party on the road and tool around a bit. Longing to be a part of this adult world, I jumped at the opportunity and made sure I hurried so I'd be ready in time. In the bathroom, I found a bottle of Avon's Here's My Heart and sprayed some on.

When Roy opened his car door, I flew into the front seat and slid over to the passenger's side. He fired a startled smile at me.

"WHAT DOES HE WANT?" ROY SHOUTED OVER THE music playing on the stereo as we sat at the lookout. "This is so dumb! Don't the police have any-thing better to do?" His dark, handsome features drew me to him even as his anger rose to challenge the Michigan highway patrolman pulling up next to us.

Moments before, the guys had lounged in their seats, bench racing and exchanging and debating car facts. My heart thumped in fear at how quickly this dream evening had crumbled to pieces.

In trouble with the law on more occasions than I could count, my brother often tucked some of his troubling issues from the family's view.

Were the police looking for Norm? He'd wanted Roy to buy the drinks on the way over. Did Roy know we were all underage?

Roy threw a brief glance at the backseat and sighed loudly enough for us to hear. He slapped the side of the steering wheel and stepped out, slamming the door. Sweat from my hands was about to drip onto my lap. I rubbed them together and hid them under my thighs.

The husky officer strode to the driver's window. "Everyone, step out one at a time and hand me your ID."

My brother pushed Roy's seat forward, opened the door, and maneuvered his way out of the car. He walked to the officer. After a moment, the officer motioned to Norm's girlfriend, and she slid across the backseat and got out through the same door. She walked over and stood next to Norm.

Even though they stood at a distance, their muffled voices carried to the car.

My mind raced. What was going on? It was only a drive!

Alone with Roy, I avoided his attention. His pulsating tap on the wheel sent my mind whirling with curiosity about what the officer was searching for.

Norm had insisted I tidy myself up and come out with them. "You can tag along, but keep quiet, and don't tell Mom where we went."

I'd leaped at the chance for an evening out. As the youngest of three, I always felt left out. A little excitement sounded pretty great. Way better than cleaning the kitchen and doing everyone's laundry.

Why had Norm even included me in his plans? Had Roy asked him to?

I stole a peek out over my shoulder. The officer motioned for me to get out. I opened the passenger door and complied.

He asked me for identification. I passed him my school ID; the only kind I had at my age. He looked it over and placed it back in my hand.

I climbed back into the car, listening to the officer's deep voice as he conversed with Roy. I kept my window down and watched their conversation through the rearview mirror.

"I've picked up on your habits, and I've noticed there's usually a part of the evening when you have a drink or two, Roy Wendel. You'll find yourself in trouble if those three were along for that kind of ride. You should reconsider who you spend your time with."

Roy's stance widened, and he puffed through pursed lips. "Don't you think, Officer, that I can ride around with whoever I want?"

"Yes. But a fourteen-year-old?" The officer shut his notebook and stuck it in a side pocket of his pants.

"No one here's fourteen. What are you lecturing me about?" Roy shot a look at the car.

"Lou is. I checked her ID. Her brother and his girlfriend are both eighteen." He smiled like he'd perceived it all before talking to us.

"That's not what they told me. Norm said that he just turned twenty-one today and that his kid sister was eighteen."

The officer put his Stetson on and strode to his car.

I was the good one. I never would have told anyone I was eighteen. I scanned the pullout ahead of us. Could I make a quick escape over the edge of the lookout? Anything to avoid the hotspot the car had become.

Roy walked to the trunk of the car, where he'd put the liquor before we left on our drive, and slammed it with a clenched fist before jumping into the driver's seat. The radio blared, and the moments I'd longed for—stealing looks at Roy as we visited —evaporated.

As soon as Roy pulled into our driveway, he unlatched his door and motioned for me to exit. My brother and girlfriend jumped out and scrambled away before Roy could say a word.

I eased out of the car, hoping to smooth things over. *Would I meet Roy again under different circumstances?* I walked around the opposite side of the car and faced the most attractive guy I'd ever met. Wow, a mature guy with his own car! How old was he? Not much older than Norm? Right?

His dark complexion made me blush, and I admired his hair, which was smoothed back like all the guys wore it. Confident and strong, he stood staunchly in place.

Yikes! His handsome light-gray eyes captured mine, and he mouthed, "Fourteen?"

I dipped my chin to my chest and looked at my feet because I couldn't hold his piercing stare. He slid his hand into his front pocket, took a step back, and flipped me a dime. I caught it and the movement delivered a chill down my spine.

"You're cute, Lou. Give me a call when you grow up." He slipped into his car and drove out of my life.

Well, for a little while.

Chapter 1

BEGINNINGS

MICHIGAN 1976

I ROSE FROM THE WATERS OF BAPTISM OUT OF THE cool lake. Blinking away the water that dripped down my face, I wiped my dark hair out of my eyes. My stylish bouffant wasn't much of a worry as I stood there, drenched.

Deep within, my soul pulsated the reminder: it's a fresh beginning.

My legs, weightless in the lake, carried me back to the shore in front of the crowd gathering to watch. The transparent water allowed me to see the polished rocks that guided me. My husband, Roy, thrust his chest out with pride. I reached for the dry towel he extended me and returned his hug.

"Thanks." I dabbed the towel at my face and felt little arms reach around my waist.

"Hey, you two!"

Our two, young kids, Rusty and Pam, squeezed me tight.

Pam moved from our family hug to an energetic bounce beside us as the church family sang the chorus of "Amazing Grace." The occasion impressed itself on my heart and set me afire from within.

Jim Fales followed me from the water, his eyes beamed bright, and he couldn't contain the smile across his broad jaw. Our pastor and friend, he'd baptized both Roy and me.

"It's hard to describe the joy it brings me to share in this day!" Jim wiped a tear from his cheek. "I am excited to see how God is going to use your—"

"I need to be the first to hug them!" Faith, Jim's fiancé, interrupted and pressed past him.

She wrapped her arms tightly around me and squeezed so tight I let out a grunt. Though I was chilled from the lake water, a warmth rose through my body. We huddled close, encircling one another.

Pam interjected and pulled at Faith's shirt. "Hug me, too!"

Faith brushed at Pam's head and drew her in. Our heads bowed, Jim led us in a prayer of thanksgiving and the joy of rebirth.

After Jim's prayer, I made my way to a small lakeside shelter to change. I tugged on Roy's soft flannel shirt and the essence of Old Spice wafted into the cramped space. I slipped into some soft pants and saw the scars on my legs. They testified to the pain of years wasted, especially since I'd never found out how I'd been hurt the night those wounds appeared.

Roy and I had spent a long time living for the moment, succumbing to whatever came along. We'd wandered from one perceived good time to the next, persuaded to join in on weekend parties with friends. The culture of the day blared the lies of free love and self-expression. We rode the wave, but it left us washed ashore.

I clasped the necklace back onto my neck and smoothed my cool hands over the front of my throat. How long had worry and fear choked my breath? In the alluring grasp of addiction, our way of living had stolen precious moments, while we slept in a stupor from nights of "fun."

It wasn't drugs that stole our lives. It was our dependence on ourselves, our belief that, somehow, we could live out life in our strength and assumed righteousness. We'd starved ourselves of genuine joy and contentment. We'd had more than our share of alcohol, and too many times, Roy had fallen asleep at the wheel...only now did I realize it was by God's grace that we were here. My new decision would prove life was worth living.

I stepped from the changing room to the bonfire, scanning the crowd for my kids. Their playful giggles could be heard from the lake, where they played with other children. The smell of campfire smoke drew me close to the dancing flames. I rubbed my palms together over the fire and surveyed our church family gathering to visit. I hadn't realized the intimacy my decision would create.

The sound of clapping startled me from my staring.

"Everyone, gather close, and Lou will share a little of her story." Jim motioned to me. He'd advised me earlier to have a short testimony prepared for the evening.

My heart argued that there wasn't a need to revisit dark details. But I was reassured by both Jim and Faith that sharing God's transformation in my life was a witness worth declaring from the rooftops! I hoped they didn't notice the trepidation the crowd caused me from my shaking hands. Roy and I had prayed a lot before our baptisms, and I was as ready as I could be. I swallowed a lump in my throat and wet my lips with my tongue.

"Roy and I married when I was sixteen," I began. "Two years later, Rusty came along. Pam came in 1970 and almost died when she was born." My eyes still burned at the memory of almost losing her. I stared into the fire and hoped no one would detect my tears. "The way we coped with the challenges we'd experienced left us hollow."

I sought a face in the crowd to calm the pounding of my heart. Faith's eyes smiled back at me, and I continued. "When a flyer about a local Sunday school blew in off the lawn, it was easy to send the kids. I let someone else watch them for a couple of hours so I could catch up on chores around the house. Then Jim came knocking at the door one day and suggested a visit with us in our home. He mentioned that our kids had asked him to come calling. He was full of joy and a gentle giant."

I glanced over at Jim, and he shrugged and looked at his feet. "He came, at first, to meet us, and then invited our whole family to church. We said yes, but we were unsure. Where did church fit in our lives? Wasn't church another crutch? We didn't need any more crutches.

"God spoke to Roy's soul that day." I paused and smiled at Roy. "Then, on Christmas Eve, he knelt down and prayed for Christ to be his LORD. Believing the gospel, he was saved from his sin. He planned to live differently. I wasn't so sure. He was my swagger-man. Untamed. I didn't think he'd change."

Roy gave me a sly smile and a wink.

I straightened my shoulders. "It shocked me. He gave up drinking and smoking cold turkey! Later, he explained how he had pleaded with God to take away those desires and then gave a testimony of how God answered his prayer.

"It's real to me because he really has changed. My husband isn't the same man." I brushed a tear from my eye before it slid down my face. "Not even two weeks later, I decided to receive Christ for myself. The difference in Roy grabbed onto me."

Faith moved across from the fire, stood next to me, and wrapped me in a side hug. She leaned swaying me back and forth. Pam moved over from where she stood and joined us.

"One day after Jesus saved me," I continued, "I was sitting in my rocker and smoking when Jim stopped in. I figured he'd talk about the cigarette in my hand, so I mentioned it first."

Jim's eyes met mine from across the crowd, and I grinned at him. "I asked him if he had something to say about my smoking. He explained to me that he believed God would impress on me His desires for my life. I was certain judgment was coming down hard from Jim, and instead, it was love—Christlike love. I saw this depth of love in him and in Faith."

Roy pulled his hand out from his pocket, placed his arm around my waist, and scanned the crowd. "I'd like to share that Lou let smoking go, but she still keeps rocking in her rocking chair!" he said.

Chuckles trickled across the fire.

"Before, she used to stay up worried about me. The kids lay awake, too, trying to wait up for me to come home." Roy used his arm to wipe his tears. "Jesus came in and changed it all! Now she rocks and sings along to the hymns we have on tape."

Roy embraced me with his powerful arms.

Across the fire, the church's music leader pulled his guitar from its case. He cleared his throat and picked at the strings. A melody formed from his rhythmic strokes. I felt my shoulders relax, and the lull from the strums impressed upon my soul the enduring peacefulness of the day.

Chapter 2

CALIBRATION

As I TUCKED THE KIDS IN BED, I SAVORED THEIR embrace and inhaled their sweet scent after a warm bath. Peace washed over me and soothed me. I tiptoed down the hall to keep the house quiet and walked over to Roy, who was sitting on the couch. I curled up next to him, nestled into a side hug, and closed my eyes with a sigh. He brushed the hair off my forehead. This day promised a bright future and newfound peace for our family.

"Lou, let's talk about going to Alaska."

The declaration sent a chill through my core like a Michigan ice storm. "With two of your friends?" I teased, hoping he wouldn't pick up the tremor in my voice.

Years ago, he had he talked about a high school dream he and some of his buddies had: a once-in-a-lifetime trip to the forty-ninth state at the world's edge. I'd read about Alaska, which promised massive mountains, vast, beautiful tundra, and a wild adventure for three teen boys.

Why was he bringing this up now?

He shook his head. "Not with friends," he said. "Al got married, and Bob says he can't leave work. Plus, I can't imagine not taking the family. The four of us can go! We'll take enough time to explore a bit and see the mountains. Breathe the fresh air. I've heard the animals are massive! Rusty would love to come across a moose. Pam will help us to remember the trip by talking about it over and over."

His excitement stirred me with questions.

"What do you think?" he asked. "Should we aim for summer? We have a couple of months to plan and prepare."

The idea didn't appeal to me. Straying from what was familiar wasn't my kind of adventure. For me, our journey meant following my man, loving him each step of the way, assisting him. I loved being his sidekick and best friend!

Adding something new? It felt too soon. We'd built our own log house together and settled in. The kids were school-aged, and we were all getting involved in the church, which was now "family." We learned under Jim's teaching what it meant to be a Christian and how to read God's word. As a newborn babe in this Christian life, I was ready for a new adventure, but I wasn't sure what great lengths I'd take to have one.

"Alaska is far away." I tried to make him see the grandiose size of the idea. "I've heard the road there is rough, and some people don't make it without losing a tire or two. They end up broken down in the middle of nowhere."

"Wow, stranded with you? Sounds great! He teased me with a playful smile. My bold man! He always cheered our family with his humor.

I pulled my legs in tight and wrapped my arms around my knees. Loneliness was a heavy weight, as I knew from my childhood. I'd endured plenty of years at home alone because my mom was more absorbed with herself and her interests than she was with me. My chest ached with the memory. I'd experienced isolation, and it didn't bring me any amount of wonder or excitement.

Yet, I experienced safety with Roy, who knew how to pull me in close and reassure my heart. I longed to embrace this exciting idea because I understood that it was something that he'd wanted to do for years. I supposed if he was excited, I could let his ambition lead my reluctant heart.

"Can we sleep on it and talk more tomorrow?" If I put the decision off a little longer, I could see whether the excitement of the day had ignited his grand plan or if it was something he really wanted to do.

He nodded at me with one movement of his head and turned off the light over the table. The room turned dark in the absence of the bulb's glow, and so did my impressions of a vacation to the edge of civilization.

THE NEXT AFTERNOON, A KNOCK ON THE FRONT DOOR stopped me as I moved from the couch. I opened the door, and Jim stood there, his arms hanging at his side. His voice thickened as he spoke. "I'm sorry, Lou."

What had dropped his gaze so low?

"Jim, what are you sorry for?"

"You and Roy." He looked into the house. "What, he's not here? Well, he stopped by this afternoon and told me."

"Jim, what are you talking about?" My head felt light.

"Oh." Surprise flashed across his entire face. His eyebrows lifted, and he gave me a stiff, clenched smile.

I was about to grab his arm and demand he tell me what brought him over when Roy drove up and parked next to Jim's yellow Camaro, instead of pulling into the garage under our house. Roy walked toward me, shook his head, and rubbed his forehead with his fingers. Rusty ran past me and jumped into his arms and Roy swayed, caught off guard. Dizzy, I held the door jamb to steady myself, and my heart pounded in my chest.

"Daddy, what's wrong?" Rusty, only seven, but observing that his daddy wasn't his sturdy self, cupped Roy's face in his hands and smiled at him.

Roy gave Rusty a shoulder squeeze, then looked deep into my eyes. "Sorry, Lou. I should have come and told you first. A tractor on the road slowed me down getting here. I'd met Jim on the corner by the church, and I let him know what was going on. They laid me off at work today." He didn't skip a beat. "Rusty have you ever learned about a thrilled moose? Or a frightened caribou?"

"No, I haven't. Where'd you see those?" Rusty darted his eyes around as if one would pop out any minute. "Did Uncle Blake catch one in a trap?"

Roy smiled big and pulled Rusty's hat over his forehead. "Da-ad!" he complained at Roy's playful gesture.

Roy twirled Rusty in the air and set him down as he walked over to me. He clasped my arm and didn't let go as he spoke. My mouth grew dry as I waited to learn how this layoff had turned from solemn to exciting.

"I stopped to tell Jim because I realized we would need prayer for wisdom, and on the way home it hit me head on!" He jumped back. "The tremendous force jolted me, and I almost ran into a tractor!"

"Daddy, no!" Pam clasped her hand over her mouth.

So amused by his own antics, Roy's voice softened. "No, I didn't get hit. However, I was slammed with the most amazing idea! Since I don't have a job, let's go to Alaska now!"

At this, Jim gave a wink, waved, and shouted over his shoulder, "I'll be back later for coffee. I want the scoop, but first I have to meet with Faith."

The blue water in the kiddie pool sparkled in the sun, and I squinted to see Roy's face better.

"What do you say?" He placed his firm hands on my waist, twirled me in the air, and landed a kiss square on my cheek.

How could I tell him no? "Of course. Let's do it." I grasped his hands and clenched them tight, hoping to infuse him with my concern. "But how can we afford this?"

"No worries, I've set money aside for some time. Building the house out of pocket was the best we could do for our stash, so now we don't have debt. Lou, we've plenty enough to enjoy a grand trip north."

Enough money indeed, but did I have sufficient grit in me to stand the test of Alaska?

AFTER CLEANING UP FROM SUPPER, I BREWED COFFEE on the stove top. I heard the rest of the family down in the garage and decided to join them. Careful not to spill anything, I eased down the stairway that led to the garage under our house. I steadied the full coffee pot to place it on the workbench, then sat on the barstool next to it and tried to see what had detained Roy's attention under the hood of our new truck.

At supper, I hadn't mentioned the gut-ache I bore over this new purchase, made so soon after he'd lost his job. Why hadn't I spoken up? With time, would Roy's carefree spirit reassure me about all these changes?

He didn't acknowledge the aroma of fresh coffee. I knew something must have held his thoughts captive, since coffee was his vice. Coming off the stepladder, he wiped the drips of oil from his calloused hands onto a rag.

"Rusty, we're calibrated for the wide-open road! This new truck has its tires ready, so it will run straight." He gestured with his arms and extended his hand outward. "The oil is clean and ready for long highway miles. It's set for the job we are going to stick it to." Roy's whistle announced a job well done.

"What else do you need to cal-il-late, Dad?" Rusty flipped his bike over and spun the front wheel.

Roy's laugh echoed off the cement floor. "It's cal-i-brate. There's only one thing left, and it's your mom." He looked at me and gave me a wink.

There it was! He won me over day by day with his new casual, playful provision. We'd spent years spinning out of control. I'd dreamed of real, normal family time. This vacation could give us that and draw us closer. Could I help make it happen?

Jim walked in through the open garage door and gave Rusty a high five. "Roy, that's one groovy truck you have there. Is it your new toolin' hot rod?"

Roy didn't answer.

"We are going to Azzzlaska!" Pam's minute hands were placed on the hips of her petite five-year-old frame. Her scolding look jetted up to Jim, who towered over her.

"Wow, Azzlaska! Sounds like a pretty place. Think you'll walk all the way, Little Pam? Or perhaps you'll ride a moose? Maybe a grizzly bear will let you ride on his back?" Teasingly, Jim curled his shoulders and let out a growl, which sent Pam out the door with a scream.

Rusty gave Jim two thumbs up. "Uncle Jim, you scared her good!" He leaned on the truck with his elbow and puffed out his chest. "We're calibrated!"

"Oh, you are? Like calibrating a gun?" Jim's question came with a glowing smile.

"You can calibrate guns?"

"Yes. And often, you can calibrate all kinds of things. Even you can calibrate, little man." Jim tousled Rusty's brown hair. "When you are calibrated, you are fine-tuned and ready to face a task. You want your daddy's truck ready, and I want my gun on standby for when I go shoot a buck this fall." He held his arms up as though he was holding an invisible gun, then looked down the barrel and pretended to fire. He kneeled down on one knee, eye-to-eye with Rusty. "God wants you calibrated, ready for how he's going to have you help Him. Yes, Rusty, I like the word. I should give a sermon about it one day." Jim smiled, flipped Rusty's miniature two-wheel bike over, and sat on it. He attempted to put one foot on the wheel, only to find himself on the floor in a flash.

Rusty laughed loud and pointed at Jim. "My bike's not calibrated for you!"

I laughed as I rose from the stool and half-jogged to the yard to look for Pam. I returned with her trailing behind me, whining about a bath she didn't want to have.

"Jim, can I get you some coffee and perhaps a slice of fresh apple pie?" I asked.

Jim jumped up from the floor, attempting to lower the kickstand on Rusty's bike. "You have pie? Well, yes, I would love some!"

I passed by Jim and grinned at Roy, who inquired with his eyes about my offer. My face felt warm to the touch as I pulled a strand of hair from my eyes. "No, Jim, I don't have pie. I just figured I'd ask if you'd like some."

I wasn't usually one for joking, but the mood was so light and amusing, I couldn't help but loosen my tamed tongue.

Chapter 3

WELCOME TO ALASKA

OUR DRIVE UP THE HIGHWAY WAS UNEVENTFUL. THE excitement pulled us north with ease. My only struggle was the edginess that brewed inside me from listening to the kids bicker on a regular basis.

At the next turn, Rusty read a sign on the side of the road out loud. *Welcome to Fortymile Country.*

"Forty miles from where, Daddy? What does that mean? Is it a long way?" Pam bounced in the back seat of the pickup.

"Stop talking, Pam," Rusty snapped back at her. "Can't you sit still already?"

She had dozed for most of the trip. *Phew!* A blessing indeed versus the incessant chatter and querying from her inquisitive five-year-old self.

Roy adjusted his rearview mirror. "I don't know, peanut. Your mom will read and find out. Lou, did you see anything about going across Fortymile country?"

"Hmm..." I searched, feathering the pages from the travel guide.

Such odd terms described this vast and impressive area that greeted visitors as the largest state in America. It didn't seem distinct from the trees or forests of the last three hundred miles. A visceral expanse of untouched and seemingly uninhabited land splayed out before us, while the mountains ebbed away to the south of us. We were enveloped in some low hills that followed the road in a snake-like fashion. Our last break was a stop for fuel in Border City: a small dot on the map right after the border entrance into the United States from Canada. The information in the travel guide I'd bought there was surprisingly limited.

"Mom, I thought when we got to Alaska, we were gonna take a picture with your new camera." Rusty squirmed forward in the seat to rest his hands on top of my head, then dabbed my beehive hairdo. "Like, ta-da! We're here!"

"You were napping and so was Pam." Roy slowed the car. "Plus, it was raining cats and dogs."

The throb in my hips made me long to walk. Sleep would be welcome when we stopped in the first town.

"Remember, Mommy, you said we'd go to a park when we got to Azzlaska. I'm going to look real hard for one."

"Pam! You're so gross. Stop licking the window! Please, Dad, can we stop and let her out!" Rusty let out a loud sigh, certain it would make us notice his annoyance.

The distance from home grew. Mile after mile, we'd proceeded through the Canadian wilderness without encountering another vehicle.

Still another twenty miles until Tok. I crossed my fingers and wished for a trip without a flat tire. I caught myself and uncrossed them. Instead, I folded my hands and expressed a mute prayer, appealing to God for peace to hold my soul instead of the concern that had sneaked into my throat.

I closed the book on my lap, since I didn't find what I was looking for. I worked to answer the kids' questions as best I could. "When we arrive in Tok, we can ask at the visitor's center," I told them, when I was out of ideas and information.

The black spruce trees covered the hillsides for hundreds of miles. I rolled my window down to let in some fresh air, believing it might lighten my mood for this last leg of the trip. Roy steered the car across the lane and turned into a gravel parking lot. A log building stood towering above the aspen.

I read the sign on a creosote pole aloud. "Miner's Road-house". This looks neat."

We pulled into the circular driveway, and as soon as the truck stopped, the door flung open. Pam's feet sprang into action.

She looked over her shoulder toward the pickup. "It's a swing!"

Placed between two large spruce trees, a swing hung in the center of the grassy island. Rusty chased her and beat her to the rope contraption. Then he rolled his eyes and gave in to her moaning for a turn first.

I stretched to reach my toes and sighed. Then I straightened up and followed Roy as he strode ahead a pace or two.

"This is grand!" he said. "Look at the width of those logs!" He passed his hand along the rounded amber logs on the side of the building. "I wonder what the story is for this ol' girl?" He squinted his eyes and peeked into a window at eye level.

"Old! Who you callin' old?"

The wooden door swung wide open and disclosed a youthful woman who rubbed her face with the floral apron tied around her waistline. She placed her hands on her hips, her eyes shining. "Come on in!" She waved us in and took a step back. "And bring your little ones!"

We followed her into the lodge. Her steps brushed against the wooden floor, drawing my eyes to her beaded slippers.

The kids ran ahead of me. Pam's wide, dark-brown eyes explored the space. Rusty beamed at the cobwebbed antler mounts that hung high on the gable-end of the living room. "Are those moose horns?"

Pam pointed to the wall at a dark hide and scrambled between Roy's legs. "Daddy, Daddy, it's a bear!"

Our cheery host flung her long yellow braid behind her back. "Welcome to Miner's Roadhouse! I'm so glad you popped in! We're not open yet, but you're welcome just the same."

She strolled to the large living room to the left of the door and motioned toward the log furniture circling a rock fireplace that rose to the rooftop. "Please make yourself at home. Do you want some fresh bread?" She clasped her flushed cheeks with her hands "Where are my manners?" Her arms extended as she knelt close to Pam. "I'm Birgit Williams. And who are you little one? Are you a little black bear cub with splendid dark hair?"

Roy returned her friendly welcome and held his hand out for a handshake "I'm Roy Wendel, this is my wife, Lou, and these are our kids, Rusty and Pam. So nice to meet you, Birgit. Not sure I've met anyone with that name before."

Birgit let out a sigh. "I presume you're tourists visiting Alaska since I've never met you before and I know everyone in town. So please accept my welcome to our great state. I'm the essence of Alaska right here in this cabin in the woods. Not boasting, no, not at all." She waved her hand back and forth. "Gosh, I can rattle on and on. I'll bring the bread right over."

She stepped across the room, brushed her hands on her apron, and picked up a wooden tray with a tall loaf of steaming bread. "My name means 'powerful or strong.'" She flexed her arm and laughed at her own antics. "My father was with the Army when they built the ALCAN. That's the golden road you most likely traveled to get here. He loved Alaska and wished to establish roots here, so he traveled home to say goodbye to family."

She set the bread on the wooden coffee table and placed napkins by the tray. "When he came back to Alaska, he devoted a couple years to traveling by boat along Alaska's inside passage, and lived in a fishing community along the way."

Birgit stood up to serve us each a piece of bread. "It's where he fell in love with my mom, the daughter of a Norwegian angler. After staying on the island of Wrangell for a bit, he brought Mom back to where his Alaska adventure started. They traveled north from Wrangell on the ferry to Haines. Once on the highway en route, barely north of Haines near the Canadian border, I was born. That's why I'm Birgit. Perhaps my parents perceived I would have to flesh out my name's meaning of strength."

She sat next to Pam on the velour couch, brushed the seat with her palm and looked around the room to study each of us. "How's the honey wheat bread?" Her query came with a bright smile that spread across her entire face.

Birgit plopped down next to Pam and Pam jumped, her bread crumbs tumbled onto the wooden plank floor.

"Birgit, thanks for welcoming us in." I helped Pam pick up the crumbs and enclosed them in a napkin. "Do you live out here by yourself?"

I couldn't imagine living there alone like Birgit did. Little cabins were strewn along the highway, but where was the community? Would she entertain strangers alone? Was she placing herself in danger?

Birgit stretched across the coffee table, took the crumpled napkin from my hand, and rose to stand next to the quilt rack behind the couch. She stroked the quilt with her fingertips, an expression of yearning crossing her face. She blinked, raised her head, and stared at me.

"I have an uncle who lives nearby. Now, let's give you the grand tour quickly. I'm sure you'd like to make it to Tok and settle in for the night. Land's sake! I didn't even ask you where you're from! Please tell me about you!" She pointed at Rusty, and his face flushed to the tips of his ears.

"Uh, I uh. I'm from Michigan, and we're on vacation. I'm hoping to find a moose, Miss Birgit. Like the one on your wall, except alive."

"I wanna see a caribou and a *wabbit*, and a whale and a..." Pam giggled when Roy gingerly bonked her on top of her head with his hand.

"Would you like a tour of the ol' place?" Birgit offered.

"We'd love to." Roy said. "Come on, squirt." Roy nudged Pam. "We read about roadhouses on our trip. There's a lot of history here." His calloused hands caressed the enormous log towering upward, which braced the second-story loft space above us.

The warm yellow sunshine sparkled on the countertop in the long kitchen. As I walked past the wood burning cookstove, I felt its heat. We followed Birgit through the rustic halls, which echoed our footsteps. What kinds of people traveled here before? What did they come to Alaska for? Or were they running far away from something?

We ended our tour at the wooden front door, which Birgit propped open with a large rock. She rested her hand on top of the oil-rubbed lock handle. "Tusen tak! That means a thousand thanks in Norwegian. Thank you for stopping in." She tousled Pam's dark head. "I hope I see you again, little bear cubby."

"Thanks again!" I said.

Hearing a suspicious hissing noise, I looked over my shoulder, stepped from the shelter of Miner's Roadhouse, and turned my head to listen closer. The sound grew louder as I neared the truck.

Roy stepped around the car and confirmed my suspicions with a nod of his head. "We've a flat tire."

"Less than twenty miles from civilization. Thank you, LORD," I whispered to myself.

The tailgate clanged down, startling me, and I made my way to the back to watch Roy loosen the spare underneath. Roy worked to switch the tires, Rusty right beside him, doing what he could to help.

Birgit's whistle pierced the silence. "Look at you! You're an old sourdough for whipping out a spare and getting back on the road. Here I thought I'd have to open the shed and pull out my tools."

"A sourdough, eh?" Roy rubbed at his greasy hands and pulled a hanky from a back pocket.

"You'll catch on to our lingo. A sourdough is someone who has spent a full winter in Alaska. Winters are long, rough, and not without a flat tire of sorts. It wouldn't be a worry for you."

Roy finished maneuvering the tires, and we climbed back into the truck. I waved goodbye to Birgit, who stood in the doorway of Miner's Roadhouse.

Roy shut his door. "Our first encounter with a bumpy Alaskan road has proved it's one we're calibrated for!"

He gripped the steering wheel and turned it hand over hand as our truck drove over the gravel driveway west onto the smoother ALCAN Highway.

Chapter 4

Tok

June 1976

Roy and I woke up before the kids and sat in the camper, flipping through the pamphlets we'd found at the visitors' center. "Tok, Alaska boasts itself as the gateway to the state." Roy sipped his coffee and flipped the page on the visitor's booklet. "Sounds like we've got two options. Continue on the ALCAN north to Fairbanks or go south toward Valdez." He stood and balanced himself to put a sock on, and the camper rocked from his sudden movement.

"It doesn't matter to me which direction we go." I hoped our trip proved to be carefree and a welcome time of rest. Roy worked so hard for our family. I knew this dream trip would refresh his spirit. We should take this time to enjoy one another.

Roy used his finger to follow the lines on the map. "No matter which way we go, we'll end up back here in Tok, since it's the way in and out of the state on the ALCAN. Looks like we are about one hundred and ten miles from the end of the ALCAN in Delta Junction. Once we get there, we'll turn onto a different highway to get to Fairbanks. It might be neat to head that way and finish this highway from end to end."

"Sounds fine to me."

"Good morning sleepy heads, start getting ready for church." Roy ruffled the kid's covers.

We'd planned on going to a small church down the paved side road.

"I'll get the bread out for toast. Can you find the apples from yesterday?" I walked to the kitchen sink and washed my hands in a basin set inside of it with water we'd hauled from the gas station. "Kids, we need to eat soon." I placed a slice in the toaster, set the dial, and took the peanut butter off the counter.

"Here's the fruit from the store. I can't believe how expensive those apples were! No wonder they're golden delicious— they're probably laced in gold dust!" He set them down and elbowed me in the side. "Can you believe it, Lou? We're here!"

"Yes, I can. The drive took forever! If not longer! My legs ache from all the sitting."

"I know it was rough for you. We're here now. You'll get to stretch your legs when we walk around town today." He squinted his nose at me and placed a gentle kiss on my forehead.

"Daddy's kissing Mommy" Pam's sing-song voice echoed in the small space. She eased herself out of bed and climbed onto Roy's lap.

"How's my bear cubby this morning? I like the little nickname Birgit gave you. It suits you so well." Roy raised an eyebrow at me. "All your dark hair." He ran his hand down the top of her head.

"And her nasty temper and that growl she has when she's hungry. Oh, yah!" Rusty climbed from the bed and gave Pam a gentle punch on the arm.

A knock on the door startled me, jolting my arm as I took the first piece of toast from the toaster.

Roy set Pam down and walked to the camper door. "Hello?" he said, as he opened it.

A thin man with glasses smiled at Roy. I stepped up beside him to get a better view of the stranger. He wore gray slacks and a sage-green button-down shirt. A bolo tie cinched his neckline.

"Hi there! I'm Fred, the pastor at Faith Chapel just down the block." He pointed down the roadway. "Dale works at the visitor's center, and he encouraged me to make sure you're invited to Sunday school."

His smile showed his white teeth, and his eyes shone a pale blue. He held his smile as he looked past me inside the camper.

"Come on over." He waved to the kids. "The service starts in fifteen minutes. I'll see you there!"

"Thank you," Roy shut the door and looked at me. "We didn't even say yes." He shrugged as he spoke. "I guess he won't take no for an answer."

Another knock, and Roy spun on his heels to open the door again.

Fred poked his head in. "And don't worry about what you wear. We don't care if you are a fancy-clothes person or a 'hey I'm a country boy in my jeans!' kind of person."

Rusty slapped his leg. "I like him! I wanna go."

"Maybe he has a little girl I can play with?" Pam jumped off her seat and landed on the camper floor with a thump.

I looked at Roy and gave him a quick closed-mouth smile while I buttered the bread. My insides squirmed at the last-minute invitation. I loved our church family in Michigan. I'd decided I needed to continue praying about church that morning and to beg God for some smiles and gracious words to say at the attention our presence was bound to bring. Small-town life was the same everywhere, especially the way tourists stuck out. This place was tiny, and the visitor's center employee had already pointed us out!

After we ate, we walked the short distance from the camper to the church.

Cars filled the parking lot. Fred greeted people at the door. As we approached, he yelled out, "Over here guys!" as he waved his arms with sweeping grandeur. "The ladies meet next door, go ahead, walk in." He pointed to a log home tucked next to the little white chapel.

Tall spruce trees provided shade from the bright sun that warmed my back. My legs climbed the wooden stairs heavily, and I knocked on the formidable wooden door to the home. Women's laughter resounded inside. The door opened, and a petite young woman smiled and stepped back for me to enter.

Get it together, girl.

Ever since I was young, walking into a group of strangers daunted me and filled me with tension. I was like a shadow in the corner: silent but present. I would try to reassure myself, but it was like pushing someone afraid of heights to the edge of the Grand Canyon.

I stepped over the threshold of the doorway, from the sunshine to the dark shadows of strangers in a shaded living room.

Cheery faces greeted me, and a woman offered me a fresh-baked muffin. I sat in a chair and quietly listened. What kind of women lived here? Were they like every other woman, or did they hold unique traits? Within a few minutes, I felt the welcome offered to me, and I settled into hearing the wisdom of women who'd traveled this road of belief ahead of me.

AFTER CHURCH, I STOOD OUTSIDE WAITING FOR MY family. Another couple met me out at their vehicle to give me

some Alaskan brochures. Roy strode out of the chapel, his Bible
in hand. "There she is." He pointed a finger at me as he walked
over, then slipped his arm around my shoulder and turned me to
face Fred.

"It's nice to officially meet you, Lou!" Standing closest to
Roy, Fred gripped my hand in a tight handshake with both of his
hands. "Our family is going on a picnic at our Bible camp.
Nothing fancy." He smiled and waved hello at a car driving past.
"I'd love to find out your Alaska plans. See you later!" He turned
and jogged to the cars in the parking lot.

"I believe I have him figured out." Roy tucked his hands in
his pockets. He'd rolled up his shirt sleeves the way he used to
when he tucked his smokes into the folds. His dark tan
contrasted with his bright shirt. "He's the Faster Pastor! I've
never met anyone so animated in all my life."

"He's real," I said. "It's not a drug or a drink. It's him. The
message he shared during church showed me how transparent
his faith is. Roy, I don't think I'm real sometimes."

"Don't fuss about it. You're authentic enough for me!"

Roy. Always sure of himself, sure of me, sure that everything
would fall into place. How'd he take it all in stride? Even after
ten years of marriage, he amazed me with his certainty. I loved
how his steady drive helped me grow in my fears. I'd played tug
of war many times with my reluctance, yet I'd seen how time
sows balance between husband and wife.

"A picnic, Mommy!" Pam ran out of the church with a young
girl close behind and barreled into my legs. "Can we go to the
picnic, please?" Her deep brown eyes pleaded for my
affirmation.

I smiled at her and brushed the bangs out of her eyes. "Of
course, it sounds like a lot of fun." I looked toward the door of
the white chapel. "Where's Rusty?"

"He's coming," said Pam. "Some man is telling him all about
how he caught a moose!"

We laughed at her antics as she snatched the air with her hands.

Seeing Roy and the kids at home at the little chapel brought a smile to my face. The family of God is everywhere!

"AFTER YOUR VACATION, THEN WHAT? YOU'RE LAID off, right?" Fred placed a hot dog on his stick and steadied his stance as he squatted near the small fire he'd built near the lake. "Have you thought about what God may have in mind for you?" He looked at Roy "Sometimes our lives take a turn as God sets something new in motion for us."

"We haven't thought much about it. We focused on getting ready to come here, and now we're just taking it all in." Roy pulled the meat off his stick and placed it in a hotdog bun.

I slid in next to Roy to put my hot dog in the fire so it would burn quickly. I loved them burnt! "We met a lady named Birgit yesterday at the Miner's Roadhouse. She seemed nice."

"Birgit Williams. She comes to church when she can. I heard she was gone for several years and plans on opening Miner's again. It's a dream come true for her to have that place shine again. She's going to need a lot of help. Imagine, darling"—Fred embraced his wife Judy with a side hug, and she looked at him expectantly—"a nice evening drive, you and me... and all the kids. We drive nice and slow, I steal a kiss..."

Judy rolled her eyes.

"We arrive at Miner's as the sun sets and have a romantic evening of pie and—"

"The cries of tired children! Yes, I can imagine, *darling*." Judy poked Fred in the side with her finger.

"Sounds like heaven!" Fred looked to the bright blue sky and closed his eyes.

Judy dipped her hand into the cooler, cracked open a pop and offered it to me. I took it from her and let the cool drink slide down my dry throat. She watched my face and posed a question. "Where are you going tomorrow?"

"I'm not sure. I suppose we'll drive the main highway roads in a circle and end up here again before our vacation is over. Roy talked about Fairbanks first, so we may arrive there for the solstice."

I didn't plan the details. I left it up to Roy. He was the adventurer, he was great at planning, and it was his dream trip, anyway. I enjoyed keeping up with the kids and their needs and absorbing all the scenery without the burden of making decisions. I looked around at the deep blue sky. "All the daylight you have in June—it's amazing."

"It is!" said Judy. "It took me a while to adjust to the differences between here and Pennsylvania. But it's growing on me. I love the summers, and so do the little ones." She pointed to her brood, who were splashing in the lake and laughing as one of them fell off the dock.

Judy stepped closer and softened her voice. "Lou, I figure we have a lot in common! I sure hope when you come back this way you stop in again at Faith Chapel and tell us how your Alaskan tour progressed. You'll see places I've never seen the five years I've lived here. We're busy with our ministry and don't take the time to explore the state. Also, the more kids we have, the harder it is to squeeze it in."

Judy tucked her hair behind her ears. "We'll travel one day. Right now, I'm content with the way things are. Most of all, I appreciate the people here. We've such rich friendships. We take turns watching one another's kids because our families aren't close by. Holidays are mixed with neighbors and friends, making the most of what we have. I enjoy how our lives intertwine with each other's."

Judy had shared a piece of what she'd grown to love. I yearned to share too and tell her that I'd noticed how quiet she was in Sunday school. She was so similar to me, and so different from Faith—the only other pastor's wife I'd met—who was so outgoing and perky.

Perhaps Judy saw how reserved I was in the corner of the living room of the parsonage, watching everyone without saying a word in class. Everyone was friendly, but the sheer number of women threw me into reserve mode. Did she perceive how I felt? Was it in groups like this, with only one other family, where she most felt like herself?

A light breeze blew the hunter-green leaves of the tall birch trees that stood majestic next to the camp cook shack. They appeared to stand watch over the camp and sway to the cheerful laughter down below.

"I guess with the breeze coming and going, the kids may be ready to get out. Lou, can you carry these towels?" Judy handed me a stack to carry, and she placed a bag with some clothes on her shoulders. Then she volunteered to launder everyone's dirty items.

The kids were in their glory, mucking around in the lake. Filthy from head to toe, with sand and tall grass on their clothes. What a mess! Their laughter carried through the summer air. Pam bent over and hugged her stomach, laughing so hard she couldn't stand. This is what they would remember: the cool, muddy lake water seeping into their shoes as they played tag and chased frogs in the shallow water. They even tried to catch little fish with their bare hands. I didn't have memories like this of my own. I was so glad we could give them this opportunity.

"I don't think they want to stop." I rubbed my shoulder and ended up brushing away a mosquito. "They haven't even noticed all these bugs."

"Let's round it up, kids." Fred approached us at the lakeside. "Since we're at camp, we might as well sing some camp songs around the fire."

More unfamiliarity resonated. I didn't grow up going to church, learning Bible stories or songs. I longed for my kids to have in their lives what was missing in mine.

Thank you, LORD, for giving my children these memories and truths of who YOU are no matter where we find ourselves.

The kids came as one big mob toward the picnic table and food near the fire. They didn't care about the dirt they'd picked along the way, which clung to their legs.

Pam gave me a squeezing hug. "Mommy, I'm so, so happy!"

I rubbed her wet shoulder. "I am too!"

Chapter 5

Go North

IT WAS EARLY MORNING, AND THE THRILL OF OUR adventure took root and brought a lightness to my chest. Our truck and the camper Roy's parents' lent us had proved to be investments I hoped would draw us continually closer as a family. Now that we were going to enjoy a full-day's drive in Alaska, we were on high alert, searching out our windows for interesting animals or scenery. What could we expect on the first full leg of our journey from Tok to Fairbanks? It was a short drive. Two hundred ten miles would only take four hours if we drove straight through.

We crossed Dry Creek sixty miles out of Tok, and that marked our initial encounter with an Alaskan-sized beast!

Rusty's deafening scream burst from the back seat, "It's a moose!" He pointed to the road, where a massive moose sauntered along the ditch and stood on the highway staring back at us. "Mom, where's your camera?" His voice quivered with excitement as he jostled in his seat and inched as close to the front of the truck as possible.

"Thank goodness we came across a cooperative moose." Roy took the camera as he rolled down his window.

Roy gave a brief grunt, and the moose's ears pulled back. The click of the Polaroid whirred it into action and startled the moose. It trotted along to the other side of the road ahead of us.

"A classic picture. I hope it turns out," Roy said, handing the camera back.

After many odd noises, the picture slowly came out from underneath the camera.

"Mommy, Mommy it was a real moose!" Pam bounced in her seat and then stood to see the picture over my shoulder. The long process of production had us gripped in suspense.

Roy drove the truck closer to the shoulder's edge and then put it in park so we could all see our first Alaska photo. A picture we could take home and show friends. Our majestic moose encounter, captured on film. The small picture came into view as the film dried, and we all held our breath as . . .

Out came a super-sized giggle from Pam as we all laid our eyes on the moose's gigantic behind, big and brown.

The kids' response was contagious, and soon the truck shook with our laughter. I rolled down the window to let some cool air in. I shook my head and smiled at Roy. "We should buy a frame for our first picture when we get to Fairbanks."

We rolled back onto the road, and I set the camera on the middle seat so it would be ready for our next Pulitzer Prize photo.

"I wonder what other animals we will see?" I said. "Remember to look for birds and caribou. Don't forget, I have your sticker books here, so you can put a sticker on any animal you spot." I leaned over the front seat and handed them each a book.

"Mommy?" Pam rubbed her eyes, teary from laughing. "I'm going to always remember this and tell my kids."

"I have no doubt."

Pam's zest for life would hopefully prove to be an enduring quality she'd share with her family one day.

Engrossed in their new books, the kids settled back in their spots. As they sat preoccupied with their prizes, I delighted in their smiles. I'd never been on a vacation growing up. I was only guessing at how to engage the kids while on the road. It seemed like I'd guessed right. Perhaps they'd hold on to the books as keepsakes at home and show family.

The new faith Roy and I had found transformed us as individuals. It had also changed our family. I wanted so much for this trip to draw us closer and help us savor everything.

"What are you pondering over there?" Roy steered with one hand, and with the other, he gave mine a squeeze.

"It's my first time on a vacation. I'm spoiled, Roy. A new truck, your parents' camper, and this stunning destination. It's a big adventure we dove into."

"I think we drove into it."

Always lighthearted. How did he do it?

Out my window, the Johnson River came into view as we crossed the bridge. Yes, we were driving into it, into the unknown, mile after mile. Maybe not only on our trip, but also in our own lives.

Roy's hand on mine soothed me. "Be anxious for nothing." His reminder with the verse from Philippians took root in my thoughts.

"Thanks." I whispered in return.

Jim had encouraged us to memorize the verse when we were first saved.

But in everything by prayer and supplication, with thanksgiving, let your requests be made known to God. It was such a pleasant reminder, but how do you enjoy today and not worry about tomorrow?

❋

MATANUSKA SUSITNA VALLEY

WE DETERMINED TO TAKE THIS PART OF THE TRIP ONE
day at a time and let the weather and our whims help us decide
where to go. We'd seen the rushing tides of the Cook Inlet, the
grandeur of Mount McKinley and the fishing crowds casting
their lines in the Kenai River. Our trip neared its end as we
meandered the Glenn Highway from Anchorage to Glennallen.
We decided to picnic at a rest stop where the Matanuska Glacier
eased alongside the Chugach Mountain Range.

Summer days were sultry in the mountains. The clouds hung
over the mountaintops and covered the majestic peaks we'd
seen earlier from a distance. Turquoise-blue ice jutted out from
the glacier bed, pointing to the gray sky. Earlier we'd stopped at
a pulloff next to the river and listened to the silt in the water as
it flowed by.

The forty-five-minute drive from Palmer was full of winding
mountainside turns, and my stomach pleaded for a break while
my head longed for fresh air.

"Mommy, take a picture of me and my stuffy!" Pam ran over
to the edge of the lookout where the last view of the Matanuska
Glacier beckoned to be captured on film.

How did Pam burst out of the truck so fast week after week
of traveling? I guessed I needed to practice gratitude for her
enthusiasm to explore and make memories all along the way.

"Of course," I said. "Hold your bear cub where I can see him
and the glacier behind you. Alright, now smile big!" I let the
Polaroid capture the memory of our glacier-side picnic. "Can I
see, can I see?" Pam echoed herself, and her bear-cub stuffy did
a jig of delight, bouncing up and down in front of her.

Roy walked over from the rig after he inspected the stability
of the camper and the truck. Each time we stopped, he walked
around the vehicle checking tires and the integrity of the tie

downs. "Pam, how about you and Rusty run up the hill!" Roy pointed to a grassy knob next to the parking lot. "Who's faster?"

"I'll beat Pam 'cause I'm super speedy." Rusty took off like a rocket, and Pam gave chase.

I let out a deep sigh. "What a memorable trip. I'm so glad you wanted us all to come. The pictures won't even compare to what we've seen with our own eyes. Like a glacier! How can you tell someone about all the colors of blue you see in it?"

"Don't worry, Pam will try." Roy walked to the front of the truck and looked closer at the hood. "It's done good. We've got a lot of miles on it already. Let's make it another hundred miles or so to Glennallen today and then go on to Valdez tomorrow?"

"Sounds fine to me. Don't forget Fred and Judy mentioned calling them from Glennallen to inform them when we'll arrive back in Tok."

"I've thought about what Fred suggested—God opening up new opportunities. This vacation is one of them. I'll call home while we're in Glennallen and let the folks know we're doing well. Harold can fill me in if he knows of any jobs around town." Roy walked to the truck and unlocked the camper door for me.

"Good idea! You should check with your brother."

Roy at least had family to check in with. My parents had passed away almost five years before. It seemed like a lifetime ago. My kids would grow up without them.

I grabbed the bag of apples I'd left in the sink along with the makings for sandwiches from the fridge.

"We can have the kids work on postcards this afternoon and send them from Glennallen." I paused and picked up a grocery sack of chips. "Roy, did you ever get a postcard in the mail growing up? I didn't."

The only mail I received addressed to me while growing up was birthday cards from my Grandma. I remembered how much she loved me and that she knew how to make me feel special and loved. Some of my first memories were of visiting her house. She'd pull out a favorite rocking chair for me to sit on, and she'd let me pick out some gum to chew. A real treat indeed! My first time in church was with her.

"My uncle sent me a couple." Roy offered his hand for me to steady myself down the stairs. "My folks are going to love getting postcards in the mail from the kids. My dad always wanted to go to Alaska."

Rusty hurled down the hill and into the side of the truck. He panted deep breaths and bent over in half. "I won....I beat that little turkey. Dad...she's fast!" He stood and continued to inhale. "Oh, good...it's lunchtime."

Roy handed Rusty a couple of camp chairs, and they set them out in a half circle that looked out at the glacier. Pam walked back from the hill and plopped into the nearest chair.

"Rusty cheats! My teacher told me you shouldn't play with cheaters, so I won't play races with him." She tucked her bear cub in next to her, then crossed her arms.

"I do not." Rusty sat in the chair farthest from her.

I looked from one kid to the next. "What's your favorite part of the trip so far?" I detoured the argument and hoped they would follow my lead.

Roy offered his first. "Well, I enjoyed the view of the ocean outside of Anchorage, since it's something I'd never seen before. I have heard about the sea from my uncle. He was in the Navy."

"I loved the animals at the zoo." Pam sprang out of her chair and took an apple out of the bag. "Mommy, what do you love about Azzlaska?"

"I love being here with you." The bond of a family. My parents hadn't shown me what it was like. I was learning to take one day at a time.

Pam rolled her eyes at me. "Mommy, it doesn't count."

"Alright, I enjoyed seeing all the waterfalls when we drove from Anchorage to Girdwood along the ocean. They're beautiful. What about you, Rusty?"

"Alaska has some neat people. Each time we stop or we visit, the people are friendly and tell me lots of hunting stories. I want to hunt in Alaska one day and get myself a huge moose." He spread his arms over his head, mimicking a large moose rack. "Mom, I know something you looked at here! The flowers on the side of the road. What did you call those over there?" He pointed to the bush close to the parking lot. In full bloom, the deep-pink flowers contrasted next to the hunter-green leaves.

"That's a wild rosebush."

"Be thinking of what you could write on your postcards for Grandpa and Grandma tonight," said Roy.

Roy made each of the kids and me a sandwich. He was such a different man from what he had been a year before. Jim had mentioned Roy's transformation, reminding me how a fundamental change happens when you're saved, and how you can see the difference in someone's behavior. For Roy, the genuine difference shone through how he cared for us.

"Thanks, Roy."

"Thanks, Daddy." Pam took a large bite of her sandwich, then sprang from her seat. She pointed at the grassy hill she and Rusty had climbed earlier. Her mouth full of food, she spoke in a garbled mumble, and I didn't catch what she said.

I scanned over to the hill behind me. A black bear cub ambled down. My heart pounded in my chest, and I gasped, clasping my mouth. I dropped my sandwich and turned to yell at the kids to get inside. Roy already held Pam, scooped up in his muscular arms.

"Run to the truck, Rusty, and don't stop!" Roy's firm voice meant serious obedience, and Rusty understood. When we were all huddled inside the cab, Roy ensured all the doors were closed. "Lou, lock your door!"

The tension in my body rose. My hair felt like it stood on end as my skin tingled. Did we dare sit and watch, or should we flee?

"But, Daddy, he's so cute. I want to pet him."

"Quiet Pam. You'll see here in a minute why we don't dare get out to visit the bear cub. Where there's a baby, the momma will lurk close by." Roy scanned the hillside with his gray eyes.

My heart beat wild in my chest. I tried to calm myself and slow my breathing. The sow appeared from the crest of the grassy hill, stood tall and sniffed the air, then fixed her stare straight ahead. Chills went down my back. Roy started the truck and took it out of park, easing along slowly. "See, there is Momma bear, and she could challenge us in a flash."

"I read bears can run faster than a quarter…"

Rusty didn't finish his thought, as the sow ran down the hill, her head down, bearing straight for our truck. Did she feel her cub was threatened?

Roy sped up and turned. "We're out of here. I don't need to scare Momma any more than we already have. Hold on, everyone."

My stomach knotted, and the skin on my arms crawled, so I rubbed them with my hands. The sow stopped at the bottom of the hill next to her baby and stared at us.

"Well, didn't we have a fun picnic?" Roy tapped his hand across the steering wheel. "Now, who wants to tell Grandma about a bear in their postcard? Or how we left our camp chairs along with lunch for the cub and its protective mom?"

Silence filled the stuffy truck. I didn't plan on telling Grandma how scared I was. The kids had just come down that hill moments before.

Oh Lord, thank you for protecting them!

"Mommy, does that count for two bear stickers?"

I laughed. "Sure, you can have two."

Chapter 6

A Turn in the Road

"Well, kiddos, we've come full circle. First, we enjoyed Fairbanks, then we went south to explore the area around Anchorage and the Kenai. After that, we headed east to Glennallen and south for Valdez. Now we're headed north back to Tok. Anyone feeling dizzy?"

"I am, Daddy. I'm dizzy 'cause I can't wait any longer!" Pam's exacerbation wasn't hard to miss as she sighed loudly.

"No need to faint from impatience because we're here and you can grab your sticker books to show your friends." I slammed the truck door to ensure it shut well and brushed dirt off my elbow from the river we'd splashed in earlier that day.

Alaska summers proved intense, and the sun beat on my head as I walked over to the church parsonage. Knowing we had friends inside eager to visit with us, the stairs were a warm welcome. Our brief visit just a couple of weeks before was enough to develop a friendship with this happy couple who had settled in Tok, Alaska. Still in awe of the closeness we found in other Christians, I questioned how God orchestrated meeting like-minded people. Did He direct us through others and not only through His word?

Rusty and Pam pushed ahead, and Pam knocked on the door.

"Welcome, Wendels!" Judy's smile greeted us as she gestured us inside. Three little blonde heads popped around the corner and waved for the kids to follow.

The soothing smell of roasting meat and potatoes filled my senses. I took off my shoes, and the cool air on my hot feet brought relief to my sore heels. "Thanks so much for inviting us for supper, Judy. What a treat to have a warm home-cooked meal." I followed Judy to the bright kitchen, where the hot sunshine blasting through the windows spread a glow across the wall.

"Have a seat in the living room." Judy motioned to the front room. "I'll just set a timer for the supper, and then I'll be right there. Fred's downstairs. And, Roy, he's fixing a pipe under the stairs."

Why did the couch look so inviting? I slumped down on it and inhaled. It was wonderful to take a break and have an evening visiting. I'd anticipated it all day. If I were home, I'd have curled up and melted into the furniture. "It is so nice to sit."

"Can I get you a pop or some water?" Judy gripped the fridge handle.

"I'd love a pop!" I rubbed the back of my neck and peeked at the thermometer on the window next to me. "No wonder I could evaporate any minute! It's close to a hundred degrees out there!"

"I know, right? It's crazy how it can get so hot here—and *so* cold in the winter. I suppose, though, that's hard to imagine now." Judy gave me the pop and opened hers as she sat across from me on a sofa chair.

"Miss Judy, Miss Judy!" Pam came from the hallway with

Judy's daughter Heidi in tow. "Want to see all my stickers?" She jumped on Judy's lap with her book.

"Of course I do!" Judy gave her a thumbs up.

I closed my eyes as I heard Pam show each sticker and tell Judy about the animals.

"I saw a caribou close to the lake, a salmon in Valdez, and an eagle in a tree!"

"It's the Wendel crew!" Fred called out as he came up the stairs. I figured this new friend had one volume, and it was loud.

As the men came into the living room, Fred turned a fan on. "Ah, now it should cool it off, I hope. Go ahead Roy, have a seat."

Roy pinched my knee as he slumped next to me on the sticky leather couch. My sweaty skin gripped the couch as I tried to move from his touch. "Hey there, mister."

"I've been praying for your trip," said Fred. "I'll hear more, but first I have something to tell you! God loves you. And I have a wonderful plan for your life!" He held his arms wide, as though he was handing us a gift to open.

As a new friend, what could he possibly have in mind for us? I straightened my shoulders against the back of the couch and stuck again to the leather underneath me.

"You don't need to go home for a job. There's one here for you!" Fred rubbed his hands together and then clasped them. He leaned forward, looking back and forth between Roy and me for an answer.

My stomach twitched, and I looked straight to Roy for a cue. He licked his lips and cleared his throat.

"Tell me what you've got." Roy tapped his foot on the floor.

I longed to escape this heat and this sudden announcement. I fanned myself with my hand and wiped the sweat from my forehead. Then I turned my head, freezing my gaze on Roy. How could he even entertain Fred by listening to the impossible? This was a vacation. We were leaving for home soon. The couch enveloped me and gripped every part of my skin that it touched. I attempted to cool myself by getting up and walking closer to the fan that stood near Roy.

Fred inched forward in his chair. "I want to encourage you, Roy, in seeking God's will for you and your family. It's amazing you ended up here after getting saved and being out of work. It's exciting wondering where God might lead. Birgit stopped in today to talk about Miner's Roadhouse, and I thought of you both. It's obvious you are talented folk who love God and his people."

I clung to Fred's words, trying to understand. I continued to fan my shirt, which wanted to cling to my back. The timer went off in the kitchen, and Judy moved to turn it off.

Fred leaned closer, a hand on one knee. "Birgit needs help—reliable, trustworthy, and knowledgeable support to run Miner's Roadhouse." Fred moved closer to the end of his seat, set his jaw and looked at Roy and me. "Want to know more?"

A closed-lipped smile came across Roy's face as his eyebrows lifted. I hoped he would talk since my head was fuzzy and I couldn't think clearly. I wanted to spring into a cold pool of water and sink to the bottom. That'd jerk me back fully into the moment.

"How about we eat first, and then we talk more over dessert?" Judy stood between the kitchen and the living room, holding a steaming pan.

Thank YOU, LORD!

The prayer settled deep into my soul. I fidgeted with my wedding ring. "Sounds great, Judy. I'll go tell the kids." I left and went to round them up. The kids formed a circle on the floor of a bedroom, peering over the sticker books.

Down the short hallway, I heard Rusty's voice over the others. "I love Alaska! And I don't want to go home to Michigan." I paused and bit my lip, then pushed the door open. "Time for supper."

Rusty looked at me, his complexion ruddy, his eyes sparkling. "Hey, Mom? Can I show everyone our pictures after supper?"

"Of course."

He sprang up and gave me a big hug before following his new friends out the bedroom door.

In his fierce hug, I felt his enthusiasm. It wasn't so long ago that he'd cried himself to sleep worried about when his Dad would come home. I needed to be strong for my kids and to listen to Fred. Was there something here for our family?

"SUPPER WAS DELICIOUS. THANKS AGAIN FOR HAVING us." I leaned back in my chair and folded the napkin on my lap in half again. Determined to not just hear with my ears, but also my soul, I sipped my water and savored the cool drink.

I'm sure there are verses, LORD, in your word that guide us in our decisions. I'll need your help!

"Thanks, Miss Judy." Pam slipped off her chair and used both hands to brush the hair off her forehead. "Azzlaska food is great!"

"You are welcome, Miss Pam." Judy nodded, a smile stretching wide across her face. "You can all go play outside on the playground. We'll come with dessert soon."

The roar of feet stampeding into the laundry room sounded like a thousand children instead of five. The door to the backyard slammed, and the room fell silent.

"Wow, that's a lot of energy." Roy stood and pushed in his chair. "They could power a compact car with what they've harnessed."

I rose from my chair and gathered a few plates to take them to the sink. Judy followed me and picked up the full coffee pot that had been perking on the stove top.

"Coffee, anyone?" She lifted the pot.

"Yes, please." Roy never turned down a cup. "We sure appreciate your hospitality. This wasn't on our radar when we wrote our to-do list for Alaska. Neither was coming across a job offer. Go ahead, Fred, tell us some more."

Fred pulled his chair in closer and folded his hand on the table. "I'd love some coffee too, my love."

Judy poured the hot coffee in his cup. Setting the mug down, he watched the steam rise from the mug and then put sugar from the bowl in his coffee. After stirring two teaspoons into his drink, he found my eyes.

"Lou, I'd like for you and Roy to go tomorrow and ask Birgit all the questions you'd like." He waved his palm at Roy. "Not to ignore you, but I bet your wife here has a million thoughts right now. I suggest you come outside with us, eat some tasty dessert, then go back to your camper tonight and pray about working for Birgit. Ask God to make it obvious what you should do. Tomorrow, we'll watch the kids while you drive out to Miner's. This might be a stepping-stone for some summer work, or perhaps it'll become long term." He shrugged and raised his hands. "Does it hurt to look around?"

LORD, I'm familiar with hurt from when I grew up, and the hurt of wrong choices. I don't want to feel it again.

Roy rested his arm around my shoulder and leaned in. "Sounds good to me. How about a date tomorrow? You and me? The open road?"

What could I say? I supposed a new day promised a fresh outlook. "Alright, I'll go."

Roy stepped into the hall. "Fred, let's finish putting that bunk bed together in the basement."

Fred grabbed his mug and walked behind Roy to the stairs. "We'll be in the dungeon when you're ready."

"Can I get those dishes done before dessert?" I searched for a rag in the sink.

"Sure, it would be great. The kids work in the kitchen, too." She stood on her tiptoes to peek out the window. "I'll let them play this evening, and I'll visit with you instead of listening to their impressions of the Incredible Hulk." Judy grinned.

I let out a quick laugh and gathered the damp tea towel from a hook on the cupboard. Judy scrubbed the dishes in the sink. Clean pots lay in the strainer; I picked them up to check if they were wet and set the dry ones aside to make room. As I turned to set the largest pot on the stove, the sweet scent of cinnamon caught my attention. I inhaled and took a step toward the oven. "Something smells delicious."

"It's a rhubarb crisp. I left it in there to warm it up. It is so much better when the vanilla ice cream melts on top." Judy closed her eyes, then opened them. "Funny how it is, when an aroma sparks a memory." A smile grew on her face. "The smell reminds me of my dad. I find being away from family the hardest part of living here."

She began rinsing the dinner plates and tucked them into the dishwasher while the sink filled with soapy water.

"I can only imagine." Our family back in Michigan always lived near one another.

"How do you feel about Fred's idea?" Judy pushed the button on the dishwasher, and it filled with water.

"I don't know yet."

The kids climbed on the playground ladder, going down the slide repeatedly. Maybe they'd fall right to sleep and Roy and I could talk.

It's the truth, right, LORD? It's true, I don't know.

"Fred is excited about it, and he's convincing when he has an idea. You'll see for yourself when you go tomorrow. I'll pray for you." Judy touched my arm with her wet hand, and the soapy bubble tingled on my skin.

"Thanks." I looked at the dish I was drying and hoped a prayer would suffice. Did God point the way? How did Christians do it? How did they know how to follow the LORD's leading?

"Let's let these dinner dishes soak. I have something to show you." Judy set the rag in the sink and walked to the living room. She picked up a notebook on a small table next to her sofa chair.

"I write out my prayer requests," she said, eyeing me. "I arrange them by the date and some brief points about the situation. Like this one here: 'Randy's leg cramps.' His legs have cramped since he was three, and I'm still asking God to help me figure out how to show patience with him when he wakes up in pain at night."

She flipped a couple of more pages. "This one has a checkmark next to it, and in red ink, I noted 'answered.' It's for a lady in Sunday school class who needed a test for a medical condition, and she was nervous. She asked us to pray for peace for her so she would accept the results with a calm heart.

"God wants to know the smallest of things which tug at our heart. I love to see how He works in my life and others.

"Tonight, I'll write your family here." She closed the book and put it back in its place, tucked by her chair.

I liked the idea. I needed this kind of wisdom that would speak peace to my mind as I detected the pain of a headache forming.

Tiptoeing out of the camper that evening, I shut the door so I wouldn't wake the kids. As I walked to my camp chair next to the picnic table, I heard the chatter of a squirrel. Roy sat in his chair, his eyes fixed on the Bible lying on his lap.

I couldn't hide the strain my entire body had endured from the exhaustion of travel, the heat, and the unanticipated announcement. Yet I wanted to sit in quiet and visit with Roy, despite the persistent pounding in my head. I lounged in my chair and set my feet on a large rock, willing myself to partner with Roy and consider this abrupt change of plans.

"The sunshine tells me it's three in the afternoon, and my watch says it's after nine." I rubbed my fingertips on my forehead and closed my eyes. "Do Alaskans ever acclimate to this daylight?"

Roy shut his Bible and placed it on the picnic table. "I'm sure it's a change each year, but they find ways to make the most of it. For example, those gardens we came across in Palmer and the pictures of the giant vegetables they grow there. The growing conditions are ideal, and they reap the harvest of the long days. If Rusty asked me, I'd tell him Alaskans calibrate to the sun each summer."

As Roy repositioned himself in his chair, he leaned over to get his mug from the table. "I thought of some things to ask Birgit when we visit Miner's tomorrow."

How do I respond with my foggy brain straining as though it's trudging through slimy mud?

"I don't know about staying. Judy says she'll pray that it's obvious what to do. It's the best I can come up with....My head is pounding."

The trees provided some shade in our camping spot, but a bright ray shone through the spindly black spruce. I squinted to look at Roy and raised my hand to cover the glare.

"Okay, let's pray, then I'll set up the icebox," he said.

"Ice box?"

"I bought a Styrofoam cooler and a bag of ice. I'll cut holes in the side of the cooler, place ice in the bottom, and set a fan on top. It'll blow air over the ice, sending cool air out the sides through the small holes, and you'll have a nice breeze to cool you off. There's an extension cord we can run to the outlet outside."

I stared at him in awe. His inventions continued to amaze

me, even after ten years. He always found a way to make things happen. I sighed, closed my eyes, then opened them to assure him with my gaze that I was grateful for his care in helping us all get a good night's sleep in this heat. "Thanks."

He took my hands in his own, and their warmth was like a gentle hug. "Our Heavenly Father, thank you for this day and for our family. I pray you will lead and guide us tomorrow at Miner's Roadhouse. Please, make it clear to us what to ask Birgit. Help our decision become obvious. We're grateful for your love for us, and we pray in Jesus' name. Amen."

"Amen."

Chapter 7

MINER'S ROADHOUSE

IS MINER'S WORTH OUR TIME AND ENERGY?

Sunshine warmed my shoulder as we followed the road east out of town. Should I warm to this idea as being led by God, or were we riding the excitement of our vacation? As we pulled into the driveway, many questions rolled through my mind, like a movie reel on fast-forward.

Roy and I walked together to the entry. "Remember to keep an open mind, Lou. Make mental notes, and pray as you look around."

"I'll try."

Birgit greeted us at Miner's. We walked in the door with fresh eyes to scan every inch of the log home. Her genuine smile lit her fair face and rosy cheeks. She stood erect and held her head high with open arms. She patted her apron where floured handprints left their mark on the pockets. "I'm glad you took the time to come and visit with me and Miner's," she said. "My house is an extension of my family, and I consider it part of my parents' heritage. Please, please come in. Can I get you a cup of coffee?"

"Thanks, I'd love some," said Roy.

"Yes, please," I answered, at the same time.

We followed Birgit through the entry and passed the living room to the open kitchen. She motioned for us to sit down at the counter. Then she went into the kitchen, took cups from a shelf near the stove, and poured us steaming coffee from the percolator on the cooktop stove.

I sipped the piping hot coffee and let it slide down my throat and warm my chest. "How long have you lived here?"

"I grew up in this house." She waved her hand in a sweeping motion. "It's all I know. My parents built it when I was a baby. They used to run Miner's as a roadhouse when I was younger. It's sat dormant now for a few years since their passing. Now it's reborn!

"Since you were here last, I opened and can't keep up with the demand." She pulled a large pan out of the oven and set in on the butcher block counter. "Word spread about fresh-baked bread and pies, and now folks from Tok are meandering here for an evening date or a morning cinnamon roll. Who would have thought fresh baking would bring someone forty miles round trip? Want a warm roll? I made them this morning for my guests."

She used a spatula to cut two of the biggest cinnamon rolls I had ever laid eyes on. Each massive roll was half the size of a loaf of bread and stood just as tall. How much flour would she need to sustain this kind of master baking?

"Oh my!" I said. "We can share. Those are huge."

"Speak for yourself!" Roy elbowed me and took his own roll as Birgit opened a glass jar of white icing and lathered it on.

"Birgit, I see how these are famous," I complimented her as I used my fork to pull apart a layer of the thick roll. "Just one of them is a meal all on its own." I took my first bite, and the sweet cinnamon melted in my mouth. "Mmm, this is good!"

"Oh, don't be shy. You can use your hands to wrestle it in if you'd like, I don't mind." She waved a napkin at me. Her dark eyes shone with delight and pride. Indeed, she must have worked hard these last two weeks.

Roy set his fork down, pulled off a piece of the roll, and opened his mouth wide to take a big bite. "So," he said, once he had swallowed, "what do you have in mind for us?"

Birgit pulled a wet rag out of the sink beneath the south-facing window. The bright yellow sunshine lit up her face. She stopped and closed her eyes, and a smile spread across her lips. "I can't get enough of these warm days!"

She wrung out the rag and wiped the counter by the pan. "I'll need help with most everything." She scrubbed a spot. "There isn't enough of me for all the work. I'll run you through a typical day, and you can visualize how you could fit into it. Sound okay?" She turned her head and looked at us with interest.

"Yes, of course." Roy set his mug on the counter. "Thanks for the coffee."

Birgit clasped her hands together. "I've a tingling up my back when I see how Miner's will live on! I hope you love him like I do and want to stay!

Miner's is a 'him,' I know it." She rolled her eyes. "I couldn't consider it as a 'her' with such a name."

As she walked around the island, she lifted her arms out for a hug and embraced me. The sweet scent of cinnamon and sugar lingered in her hair that was braided in a coil on top of her head as though she wore a crown.

"Miner's is one of many roadhouses in Alaska," she said. "They sprang up out of thin air out of necessity. Each one is characterized by its unique location and the provisions it offers. Here, we serve clients any meal of the day. I always have something in the oven. There are three cabins out back and two rooms in the main house, so we can accommodate up to ten people.

"The fuel tanks arrived a couple of days ago. The fuel was hauled in and pumped into tanks I already own. I have a hand pump arranged for pumping a gallon or two if someone needs it. This past week, a man asked me if I changed oil. I impressed him. I told him, 'I sure do! However, you'll have to wait for me to put on a different apron.' He about fell over!" She wiped her hands on the apron around her waist and fussed with a strand of hair on her forehead. "When you are an Alaskan wild rose, you learn how to do it all!"

I couldn't imagine growing up in the Alaskan wilderness. What caliber of a woman could do what she did? I wasn't about to compare our capabilities of holding down a roadhouse. But we could ease in alongside her and follow her lead. With her there to guide and show us how to assist, I knew Roy and I would make a powerful team.

"A typical day begins with early rising to start the bread and rolls and have breakfast ready for any guests. Then I move onto cleaning. I have rooms and laundry done by midmorning if possible. Next, it's on to getting lunch ready and hot in the oven, waiting. After that, I do some light housework, then I go into the yard to finish the outside chores, too. If I have a wild hair, I zip into town to run an errand. It doesn't happen too often."

She placed a hand over her heart. "I'm getting tired talking about all I do. Later, I start supper and loiter around, fixing things or helping those who stop in for a coffee. Oh, and there're pies to make in there somewhere. I stop serving supper and dessert by seven, so I have time to clean the kitchen before bed and lock up at nine. I need a few moments to unwind. Maybe if you're here, we'd stay up later since many hands make light work. You know how it goes!" Birgit shrugged.

"What do you suppose I'd work on?" Roy sauntered into the living room, gazing at the shoulder mount of a moose on display.

"I'm so glad you asked! Follow me outside."

We walked through the kitchen and a large pantry to another door that opened to the backyard. Our first tour, when we arrived in Alaska, hadn't included the yard, which featured roughly two acres of beautifully tilled dirt, and medium-sized plants popping out of the ground.

"My Mount McKinley-sized garden is something I hope your kids will jump right into," Brigit said. There are weeds to pull and watering and harvesting to do. And we'll stay busy canning and gathering for the winter." Birgit walked alongside the house to cement stairs leading to a door. "This is the root cellar. You can access it inside from the basement. I still have last year's potatoes, canned carrots, beets, and lots of dried herbs."

We moved past the stairway and walked down a path that led us to a large woodpile. Showcasing the supply with her framed hands, she looked at Roy. "You'll shine here! We need wood for the cookstove and the stove in the basement. Also, there's a stove in the shop. I buy slab wood from a local mill and burn it in the winter to take the bite off the chill." Birgit elbowed me. "He'll make a better burly wood chopper than me. And your son is old enough to work moving wood."

"You have a lot of wood. How much is here?" Roy scanned the pile and walked along the side of it. I could see him make his own mental calculations as he mumbled to himself.

"I have friends up the road who harvest this wood for me every year. They bring me three loads of ten cords a piece. I've used only a little since spring, so you are looking at around twenty-nine cords. It's enough for the next year, and it's good to have extra. I'm Alaskan-grown, but I'm not built for wood chopping."

Good grief, this well-equipped woman could handle herself!

Her parents were tutors in how to survive rural Alaska and make the most of the land. I could never hope to be like her. Raised in a small town, I learned how to grocery shop wisely and to stretch a dollar, but growing a garden? Harvesting? Canning? I'd have to learn a lot. Would we seem more of a hindrance to her if we needed teaching or help? Roy wasn't a stranger to bucking wood or hard work. He could tackle almost anything.

"I've saved the best for last. One more stop."

Her skirt swayed as she walked, and she hummed to herself as she led us around the side of the house and over to a log garage. We followed her into the three-bay garage.

"I'll change oil, a tire, and maybe a headlight, but the rest isn't my thing. I saw how you whipped your spare tire out and changed it at lightning speed when you were here. Will you do some wrenching if a customer needs it? I have lots of my dad's tools over in the toolbox."

A smile spread across Roy's face. He was at home in a garage, elbows-deep in a project. "I'd be happy to."

"There you have it! Miner's in all its glory. Oh, I forgot to show you the cabins out back. They're simple, and the guests use the charming outhouse nestled between them. I bet even Little Pam could wrestle sheets onto the bed and toss them in the washer when they need changing."

Birgit gathered invisible sheets into her arms and then threw them as she spoke. Her antics were impressive and engaging. I was sure guests enjoyed her charisma.

"And you, my dear Lou, you're well-suited to be my sidekick, working alongside me with meals, groceries, and cleaning. I'll do the ordering for the food and the business end."

I looked at Roy to search his face for clues of what might be at the forefront of his thoughts. He was still smiling at Birgit's rendition of tossing the sheets. Maybe he pictured Pam with an armload of laundry, stuffing it through a doorway into the house. I sure could.

"Thanks for the tour," he said. "We'll pray about it and get back with you." Roy extended his arm to shake Birgit's hand. She waved him off and went for a side hug.

"I didn't tell you anything about where you would live or what I would pay you!" She smacked her forehead. "You'll stay in half of the upstairs, with two bedrooms and an adjoining bathroom. I'll move downstairs to the nook off the living room. We'll still have the rooms for the guests, which gives your family your own space. I'll pay you whatever you earned at your last job, plus give you a percentage of what the roadhouse brings in. My offer includes your room and board." Birgit leaned toward me and placed her hand on my shoulder. "And I will be forever grateful!"

Roy shut his door and rolled down the window. His elbow rested on the opening. "We'll call."

The truck moved forward, and I tried to move my thoughts in a positive direction.

"Well? Is it obvious?" he asked, after a moment of silent driving.

I hesitated. Could I say yes right away? I needed certainty. Instead of answering, I asked, "How about you?"

"I think it's great. We can live simply, help Birgit, and make a living. It'll give us a taste of Alaska. And what a great place for the kids!" Roy looked in the rearview mirror and adjusted it.

I cleared my throat and then bit my bottom lip. *Where was my Chapstick?* I opened my purse, pulled it out, and slathered it on, using the mirror tucked in the visor. Would we be safe out here away from town? What about the people coming and going?

It was a beautiful spot and a once-in-a-lifetime opportunity. It wasn't like Roy had work waiting at home. I smoothed my left forearm with my right hand and then tucked my hand under my leg. "Could we try it? Maybe work for her two weeks at a time?"

"Lou, that wouldn't be fair to her. If we decide to do this, we'd have to stay until the end of the summer. She'll stay busy through the middle of September. She wouldn't gain anything if we left her hanging twice a month. It's all or nothing."

Wow, the heat in the truck stifled my breathing. I rolled the window down and fanned my face. Could we work enough to make it worth it? I'd need to learn fast.

"Alright," said Roy. "If you're willing to try for a couple of weeks, then I say we commit to the rest of the summer. It isn't a long time. We can catch the fall colors as we go home." He held my hand and clasped it.

His touch reassured me he would stay by me. Roy thought we could do it. Maybe we could.

"Okay, it's worth a try."

Oh, LORD, make me brave for my family.

Chapter 8

ROUTINE

WE'D MADE MINER'S OUR OWN AFTER TWO WEEKS OF diving in full steam ahead. One afternoon, I stood near the kitchen screen door, which ushered in a welcome breeze. The full day of ninety-degree weather had left me exhausted. Roy suggested we read the history of roadhouses in Alaska together as a family so we could answer questions from inquiring guests. Rusty proposed we "disguise" ourselves as Alaskans and act the part.

"Is there a Daniel Boone hat 'round here?" He peeked behind the couch and then a side table. "I'll look the part, Mom."

"Except there aren't raccoons here," Roy said. "You'll have to ask Birgit if they've something similar you could wear on your head, but you'd sweat it right off in this heat." Roy teased Rusty with a tug at his shirt as he walked past.

"I know what you can wear! A porcupine!" Pam roared with laughter and slapped her leg.

"Funny." Rusty cooled his voice and laid on the floor. "So,

you said guys from way back over a hundred years ago came up hunting for gold? Did they find any?"

Roy turned the page of the book on his lap. I sat next to him and kept my distance. Sweat was dripping off me. I fanned my face with my apron.

"They sure did! They forged trails, walking between the small towns that popped up. Pretty soon, they pulled wagons on the trails, and then in 1951, they finished the trails as a road: the Taylor Highway. The highway goes toward Eagle and extends over into Canada close to Dawson City—known for its Klondike-era attractions. The whole area north of here bustled with activity during the Klondike Gold Rush. Even now, there are still claims that folks draw gold from. There is so much history here."

I wasn't much for history, but our stay at Miner's made it come alive.

Still, I wouldn't have wanted to follow my man to Alaska in the late 1800s. Women would have been scarce, and it would have meant rough living conditions. *Imagine, no running water.* Nope, I didn't want to imagine it at all.

I walked back to stand in front of the screen door so the breeze would blow across my hot skin.

We'd settled into the routine of the roadhouse. The kids worked a lot outside, and the tourists kept pouring in, looking for a home-cooked meal. Good rumors had spread along the ALCAN, and now Miner's regularly welcomed truckers stopping in for coffee and a cinnamon roll.

Birgit suggested we host an extra-special meal once a week and encourage Tok folks to come out for supper and have home-made pies for dessert. Those were busy days. Often, I was the afternoon pie-baker, lining out the jars of fruit and making pie crust in bulk.

One afternoon was particularly busy, and I had worked nonstop. Finally, there was a lull. I rubbed my right shoulder with my left hand to ease the ache from exercising my upper body as I rolled out all the pie dough. I leaned on the door frame, my eyes closed, trying to savor the break in work.

"Wake up there, lady." A voice jerked me out of my moment of solace. I stepped aside to see a tall man standing in the doorway, a half-smile across his lips. "May I come in?"

"Yes, of course," I said. "We're open for another hour. How can I help you?"

"You must be new." His eyes scanned me from the top of my head to my toes and back to my face.

He irritated me right away. Who was this man?

The kids were chattering in the living room about beaver pelts, and their voices quieted when the man entered Miner's. It wasn't odd to have a late-evening guest, like a lone man driving a truck and hoping for some food before a nap alongside the road. But something about this man felt different.

"I always visit the first of the month." He nodded at Roy and the kids and sauntered to the kitchen. He sat down on a stool, then removed his filthy hat and set it on his knees. "Huh, looks like the Brady Bunch."

Roy must not have heard him, or he would have addressed the rude comment. I couldn't help but stare at the man who had so arrogantly strolled in and made himself at home. But I caught my attitude, smoothed my apron, and went to the opposite side of the counter.

I forced a quick smile. "Can I get you something? Perhaps a cup of coffee?" I turned to get the coffee pot off the cookstove but stopped, remembering I'd moved it earlier.

"Huh. You're new at this, aren't you." He glared at me with dark, sullen eyes, and my neck went ice cold, even though moments before I was laced in sweat.

"When I come here, I have my usual. I don't suppose anyone left you a note, so you'd know what to do?" he said.

His kind was familiar to me. I'd lived with someone like this before. My brother, who always imposed his wants on me and pushed me around. Who'd grab at my arms and make me say yes to washing his disgusting socks. His behavior led him real far in life. Right into jail—more than once.

Pleasant people didn't treat people with such disdain, lording themselves over others. This man was cruel, I could tell. I paused and hoped I looked strong, holding my ground and not cowering. Roy's presence in the living room brought me hope that the situation would not escalate.

"There aren't any notes about how to treat specific guests," I said. "I'm happy to serve you the usual if you'll let me know what it is." I wished for a reason to leave this man to himself to eat or drink; I would find somewhere else to go.

"Lady, I own this place." He brushed his hands of invisible crumbs and then crossed his arms across his chest, staking his claim. "Tonight, I'll just have a cup of coffee and leave." He squinted glaring eyes that tried to pierce my soul. "I'll let you figure out how to address guests, and then I'll come again sometime. Uh, I don't believe you ever gave me your name?"

I stepped back forcefully, as though someone had pushed me, and I hit my hip against the stove. Startled, I froze. I blinked, forgetting why I had moved back.

Yes, the coffee.

I slipped the oven mitt on and turned around, glad to escape his glare. Who was he? Why had he found his way here? He owned Miner's? I poured the coffee and stared at the cup, mesmerized by the black brew. I handed it to him without looking at his face.

He took the mug from me, and his calloused hand slid over mine. He clenched my hand firmly for one long second, then let go. I wanted to throw up in his coffee and kick him out the door. I turned to set the coffeepot back on the hot stove, and when I turned back, he was gone.

I needed fresh air to calm my heart, which raced out of

control. I braced myself on the counter and leaned in for support. Roy and the kids were snickering at something. They hadn't noticed my interaction with the stranger.

Oh, LORD, please still my reeling thoughts. Please calm me deep within. Help me, LORD.

I didn't want to alarm the kids. Maybe if I preoccupied myself with the dishes, they wouldn't notice my shaking, or the weakness that I sensed in my knees. I ran my hands under the warm water and hoped to wash away the image of the alarming guest. *Wait!* He'd taken the mug with him. I twisted on my heels and searched for the mug in the kitchen.

"They're here, Mommy!" Pam skipped back and forth between the kitchen and living room. "My friends, my friends!"

Roy stood and smiled proudly at me. I must have missed something. I didn't have a clue what was going on.

In walked Judy and her five towheaded kids. Noise erupted and giggles filled the hot air. She strode right to me and squeezed me tight. "Surprise! We're here to help with baking and anything else that will wear my kids out! Roy assured me you wouldn't shoo me away."

Roy winked at me. "Come on, out we go. I'll show you the wood pile you can tackle. Let's see how tough you Alaskan boys are."

The screen door slammed, and silence filled the room. Tears welled up in my eyes and stung. Like a wave crashing into me, leaving me limp. I grasped Judy's elbows and looked deep into her eyes. I steadied myself and held her. "You have the most perfect timing!"

"Let's give God the glory. He impressed on me this afternoon that I needed to come over. Roy told me at the store on Monday how hard you're working, and that if I ever came, you'd let me tag along. I took it as a nudge, but today it was a push by the Holy Spirit."

I let out a deep sigh. "Well, it came to you just in time!

Could we sit for a minute? If you don't mind."

Judy nodded.

I walked to the couch and plopped down. "Working here has been great. We're loving it. The kids are having a blast and don't want to go home.

"Birgit made a trip to Fairbanks for supplies, and Roy and I kept up here. It's been tiring, but fun. We've managed really well. But a strange, hostile man came in just now and declared he owned the place. Before I could ask him anything, he left. It scared me. I haven't even had a chance to talk to Roy about it yet. It left me shocked because I thought Birgit owned Miner's and also...he...he seemed so odd, and so mean." I waved my hand at her as though swatting a bug away. "Maybe I imagined it being worse than it was since I'm so tired and the heat is weighing me down today."

Judy stared at me. She was such a superb listener—the way she studied my eyes and allowed me time to finish.

"I believe you," she said. "Tell Roy so he'll watch out for him. You must ask Birgit about the whole thing when she arrives back. Now, tell me how I can best support you tonight." She stretched out her arm to lift me and playfully nudged me toward the kitchen. "Is it dishes? Laundry? Picking raspberries? Rubbing your sore feet?"

She didn't let me answer. She just went right to the kitchen sink and turned the water on. "Sit, I've got this."

I didn't argue; I pulled out a stool. "Thanks, Judy."

"I also wanted to invite you to Ladies' Tea on Saturday at the church. Some ladies from Glennallen are also coming, and we will plan a ladies' retreat this fall. I sure hope you can come. I'd love for you to meet everyone."

"Judy, I can't leave. Weekends are overly busy, and Birgit isn't coming back until Saturday evening. As soon as she gets here, we'll put everything away and get ready for the hustle of Sunday afternoon." I played with the cloth napkin, which I folded and placed in the middle of the table with a Mason jar of wildflowers.

"I understand. If plans change, come on in. The ladies will meet around one." Judy removed the dishes from the rack and set them on the counter. There weren't many. She pulled out some larger pots and sat them upside down on a towel. "I'll let these air-dry." She threw the wrung-out cloth at me. "Now show me where we can put this thing in the wash."

I caught the rag and smiled back at her. The experienced-mom ploy she used worked well—making light work of a few tasks, while getting other helpers to jump on board. I'd have to watch for clues on how to master it.

I WIGGLED THE WINDOW OPEN IN OUR ROOM. WHY hadn't I come up earlier and propped it open to cool the room off? Alaskan summer nights presented a specific challenge. How do you keep the window and its coverings open to cool the room *and* keep the sunlight out?

I pulled the curtains closed, bunched them on the upper part of the window, and tucked them in so they wouldn't blow loose. The intense Alaskan heat was unlike the warm humidity of Michigan. The sun shone almost twenty-four hours a day, creating a relentless heat you couldn't outrun or escape!

Roy shook the sheet on top of him. "I'm not sure I could handle this place if the bugs were horrible. How would we even sleep if we needed the window shut?"

"It was nice of Judy to come today. Thanks for suggesting it."

"Um-hmm." Silence fell over the room.

I continued to change into my night clothes, then sat on the edge of the bed to massage my feet.

I knew Roy wasn't a fan of dishes or working in the kitchen. Fair enough: I had no plans to work alongside him in the garage or to split wood. Our teamwork was more efficient when we divided and conquered. But his thoughtfulness in inviting a friend to come help cheer me on as I tackled the challenges of Miner's flattered me.

I slid under the sheet and laid my head on the bed. Was the pillow softer tonight? Did the bed invite me more than other nights? Calmness washed over me, and the ache in my feet eased. I closed my eyes and breathed in through my nose to smell the fresh Alaskan air. The leaves of the aspen rustled a lullaby of peaceful dreams.

At a few points during the evening, I'd run through my mind how to tell Roy about the mysterious stranger. Why did I fear being tongue-tied? Roy always supported me.

I gulped and started to share with Roy about the frightening man who had come into Miner's that evening. But then Roy's snore wafted through the air and echoed in the small room.

How did someone fall asleep instantly? Early in our marriage, Roy's dad informed me that Wendel men fell asleep at lightning speed since they didn't have a guilty conscience to keep them awake! Well, nice for them. I rolled over onto my back and stared at the yellowed tongue-and-groove pine ceiling. My eyes closed easily as the weariness from a full day washed over me.

A verse from the book of Matthew came to mind. Something about how each day was sufficient of its own problems.

Tomorrow promised a new beginning. I'd cling to a bright outlook during my daily routine, including how to handle disturbing guests. And I'd tell Roy tomorrow and leave it, for now, with the LORD, who knew far more than I did! A relationship with God, where I could literally place worries at his feet, was a welcome mindset I never could have imagined before He came into my life.

Good night, LORD. Thank you for sending a friend when I needed one. And thank you for Roy, even though he falls asleep way too quick.

Chapter 9

TRUCKERS

"JUDY CAME AND PICKED UP THE KIDS WHILE YOU were switching sheets in the cabin," said Roy. "She'll have them back at eight. I'm headed to the border to contact the man who owns the chickens Birgit wants. It shouldn't take too long, but it's close to seventy miles one way, and I heard there is a forest fire next to the road. I don't know if it will affect traffic. There aren't truckers in from the east yet, so maybe you'll have a quiet morning."

Roy gave me a quick glance and snagged a cinnamon roll from the pan on the counter. "Mmm, these are magnificent." He zipped around into the kitchen and kissed me three times, one peck after the other.

I brushed my hands on my apron and waved to him as he left out the front. The screen slammed shut. I poured myself a cup of coffee and sauntered over to the living room. I hoped for a wonderful day of silence. No talking, no whining, no current visitors—since they'd all hustled out early that morning. Today it was Miner's and me, with the whole day all to ourselves.

Birgit wasn't even there. She'd spun in from her trip late, only to quickly head up north to Eagle, where she'd agreed to bring supplies to friends. Unfortunately, there wasn't a moment to ask about the supposed owner of Miner's.

I moved the ottoman close to the couch and propped my feet up, reveling in the possibility of some rest and daydreaming instead of serving and cleaning.

In spite of all my early misgivings, our time at Miner's had turned out to be a unique gift. What a vacation! I wouldn't have dreamed of a working trip to Alaska. It had never crossed my mind. Now I thought everyone should tour this way. Instead of seeing the sights, live the life!

The smell of wood smoke caught my nose, and I sneezed. Did Roy leave something in the garage stove burning? I moved to the door and stepped outside. Looking to the east and saw a dark, smoky plume rising high into the air. It reminded me of a Michigan tornado, the way it darkened the sky. Was it from the forest fire Roy had mentioned? I wouldn't spend any more time than I had to outdoors for the day.

I brushed the tips of some fireweed that grew close to the house. The bright pink flowers swayed in the wind. Birgit had taught us about this plant. As the summer carried on, the flower buds would open from the bottom to the top. Afterward, they would morph like dandelion weeds, sending their seed as fluff into the air. Such an amazing process.

Birgit explained that the flowers' blooming progress revealed how much summer remained, and that some people believed their height gave insight into the amount of snow we would have. I guess we'd see, wouldn't we? Lord willing, we'd be there long enough to watch the flowers change.

I looked up as I felt the rumble of a Jake Break from a rig. It was early for a trucker to stop. Their usual routine was an evening-coffee turn-and-burn.

I went inside, figuring the rumbling brakes signaled a trucker who pulled over to check his load. I needed to thaw some burger meat for the night's chili, so I meandered through to kitchen to the pantry where the large freezer stood.

Thankfully, Birgit had made a huge meat purchase, hoping the supply would last into August. I picked up the note pad she used to keep track of how much food was purchased and how much was used and noted the amount I removed from the freezer. There was a noise in the kitchen, so I walked through the doorway. Four men sat on stools, all with big smiles on their faces.

"Howdy, ma'am." A man on the left spoke. "Sorry to startle you. Your sign says open." He nodded at me. His cheerfulness spread out with a kind smile. "On the CB, they said that from the chicken coop there're ground clouds ahead without a hole in the wall to see through. There's a land yacht dead pedaling, and a garbage hauler told us the cars have to hitchhike to see. My neighbors and I want to keep it shiny side up, so here we are!"

I stared at him blankly. Was that English? I raised my eyebrows but didn't say anything, not wishing to sound rude to this jovial man and his "neighbors."

From the far right of the counter, one of the men rose from his stool. "Ted, you need to lay off the CB lingo and talk American to this lady. She doesn't have a clue what you said." He stretched out his arm to shake my hand. "Ma'am, I'm Joey. This is Mike, Rod, and Ted over there. And I'll let him try again."

They seemed nice enough, and I was eager to know what was going on.

"Sorry, ma'am. All these hours on the CB, chattin' back and forth, not thinkin' about what we say because we're all known' what it is."

He gestured to his "neighbors."

"We heard on the CB from the weigh station there's fog to the ground without even an opening to see through. People are driving real slow. A vegetable hauler told us the cars are tailgating in order see. My fellow trucker drivers and myself want to arrive safe, so we thought we'd stop in. There's the American version of the story, ma'am." He nodded again.

"I get it!" I returned the gesture and smiled. "Gentlemen, if you'll give me a minute, I'll pour some coffee and serve some cinnamon rolls. We don't have a meal ready yet. Chili is on the menu tonight. I suppose I could make it for lunch if you have time to wait." I brushed my palms on my apron and washed up in the sink.

"We've heard of your chili. Miner's has a reputation from Dawson Creek all the way to Fairbanks. I hope you have a big pot!" Joey took off his ball cap.

I removed the mugs from their hooks next to the stove and placed them nearby, then poured their coffee, put sugar cubes on the counter, and brought cream from the fridge. The quiet morning I'd dreamed of was over, and I'd need to cater to the truckers.

"I don't like chili." A driver spoke as my back was turned. "Never had a bowl that made me want more. But we've been told tales of those cinnamon rolls, and they sound like near heaven."

I grabbed two full coffee mugs and shifted to face the men. I placed the cups on the clean counter and turned for the others.

Afterward, I planted my hands on my hips and watched them doctor their coffee. "Sir, I hope to prove you wrong about the chili," I said.

I went to the oven and brought out a generous pan full of cinnamon rolls, which I covered with a tea towel so they wouldn't dry out. I set the pan on the counter and lifted the cloth. You would have thought I'd revealed a gold nugget the way they all gasped. "Butter or icing, gentlemen?"

Ted raised his hand. "I'm going to have to put a big star on this mile marker on my swindle sheet." He spoke with excitement and rubbed his hands together.

"There you go rambling CB again, Ted!" Joey shook his head and rolled his eyes. "He means he's going to mark Miner's down in his logbook. Don't mind him. And thank you, ma'am."

"You can call me, Lou." I filled the sink with warm water. I'd have to thaw the meat quickly. Hungry, grown men could eat a lot. If they were bored with waiting, they might not even consider how much they consumed.

Low growls filled the kitchen as the men ate the rolls without a word.

After I topped the sink with water, I set the meat in it, then went to the pantry to look for the biggest cast-iron skillet I had. I'd need onions and green peppers too, so I placed them in the skillet to carry them. Thankfully, Birgit had canned tomatoes from her garden the year before. They proved handy for a quick meal.

I tried to think of small talk to have with the men. Too much silence might seem awkward. "What are you hauling?"

"Toothpicks." Ted stated matter-of-factly.

A laugh exploded out of my mouth. "You are hauling semi loads of toothpicks?"

Mike slapped the counter. "Ted!"

His mouth full of food, Ted shrugged.

"Lumber, ma'am, we are haulin' lumber. It's CB talk again, and I suppose Ted here needs a full-time interpreter. Ted? Whatever do you do when you're home? Can your wife understand you?" Mike rolled his eyes and gave Ted a playful shove. "We're supposed to take it to Border City, but with the smoke, I don't know when the road will open as passable."

Their forks scraped the plates clean of the icing, and they licked their lips. Mike stood from his stool. "Would it be alright, ma'am, if you kept a tab for what we eat today and let us even up at the end? And, if you don't mind, I'd like to sit in the living room."

"You can keep a tab. Please make yourself at home. It's what

Miner's is all about. What you need while on the road, whether it's a meal or a place to sit out a storm. Or, in this case, some smoke." I went and picked up one of the kids' books off a chair and placed it on the coffee table. "Sit anywhere you like. I'll keep busy in the kitchen. Holler if you need something. The bathroom is down the hall, and there's fresh water in those coolers." I pointed toward the table, where glass jars sat, and underneath lay a Styrofoam cooler full of ice.

Solace at Miner's was unrealistic.

Roy's whistle carried into Miner's, and I took in a deep breath. Help had arrived. I looked out the screen door. He casually swung the keys in his hand as he looked at the sky. He lowered his head and caught my gaze.

"I've never seen anything like it before. I didn't get far. The road is closed." He waved at the trucks lined up in the driveway. "Looks like they knew better than me. How many you have in there?"

"Four, and I don't know how long they'll stay."

"I'll throw on an apron if I need to." His eyes widened.

Was he drawing me to believe he meant it, or was it a tease?

"Um-hmm, sure you will. Thanks for the offer." I raised my eyebrows playfully at him, placed my hands on my hips, and looked him over from head to toe. "Just like I'll offer to check the tire pressure on these big rigs after I flip the bacon tomorrow morning!"

"See, there's hope for you, Lou!"

I went to give him a jab with my finger, but he grabbed my hand gently and twisted it behind my back. He followed up the playful gesture by scooping me into his arms, catching me totally off guard.

"Roy, you're going to drop me!" I said, laughing and blushing at his flirtation.

He held me tight as he fumbled to open the door.

"Good morning to you!" Roy nodded at the truckers, whose

gazes followed us in the room. He set me down and patted my shoulder. "Thanks for the warm welcome, lady!"

Ted stood and walked over to me, his eyes darting to Roy. "Ma'am, do you know this man?"

I pulled my apron off, not taking my eyes off Roy. "Yes, Ted. He's my husband." I darted at my chance and whipped toward Roy. I caught his arm with a snap of the end of my apron, whooping in delight as I beat him at his own game.

Ted set his eyes wide and placed his hands on his lap. "Yes, ma'am."

I STIRRED THE OVERSIZED POT ON THE STOVE. STEAM rose and wafted a spicy aroma into the kitchen. Was it enough chili for the guests who kept trickling in? Two more truckers had arrived later in the afternoon, along with a family of four who'd made a reservation for a cabin out back. I slid over and opened the oven door to peek at the corn bread, which cracked perfectly in the middle, just as it should.

"I found them!" Roy came from the pantry with Mason jars of the canned fruit I'd asked for. "Didn't Birgit mention these earlier? Which ones do you want?"

"How about the applesauce? It looks good." I tapped on the lids with my finger and gave the chili another stir with a large wooden spoon. "It's almost ready."

I looked at my watch, which read five-thirty. Might as well get started serving up supper since it might take longer with more guests tonight than usual. An evening crew usually sauntered in for coffee, muffins, leftover cinnamon rolls, or even a late supper, and we had to account for that. The road closure could mean more overnight clients as well.

"I'll open the jars for you, then I need to check to see if the fuel setup is ready in case any of the forest fire crew comes here needing gas for their saws," said Roy. "I thought of it earlier."

Roy unscrewed the lids and then situated them in a tidy row on the counter. He'd make a decent cook if he ever tried. His methodical ways would be handy in the kitchen.

"I'll be back." He left out through the pantry door as I grabbed my oven mitts.

I removed the corn bread and cleared my throat. "Supper is ready."

Getting through this day meant finding industrious methods of providing food and anticipating the needs of travelers—maybe even firefighters. Normally, I'd shy away from all the unexpected changes, but these challenges invigorated me to see the evening through. Miner's seemed like home right now, and I felt safe under its cover.

Ted hopped up from his spot on the couch. He looked back and forth across the room. "Ma'am, I'd love to have some of your chili. I've been pining for it all day." He pulled out a stool and placed a Mason jar glass he carried with him on the counter.

The other truckers followed him. I filled bowl after bowl and set them out for visitors, then cut pieces of corn bread to pass out. I gazed around at the faces of the crowd that had formed in front of me.

"This isn't our usual setup, so I'll put these out for you to help yourself. I trust you'll be honest with me later about what you ate when it comes time to tally your tab. There's a ledger here on the counter. Chili and corn bread with a side of applesauce is two fifty. Please let me know after supper if you need a room." I pulled out spoons and placed them upside down in a pint-sized Mason jar, then gathered napkins to place next to them. "Oh, and don't forget there is cold water here by the hall."

I wiped my hands on my apron and watched as, one by one, they picked out a bowl. I decided to soak a couple of dishes.

"Ma'am, this here is the tastiest chili this side of Canada."
Ted held a spoon and smiled wide. The other truckers took their
meal to the living room, where I had placed T.V. trays earlier.

Thankfully, the kids would come home after the busy part of
the day. I didn't have much longer to go before I could wash the
dishes. I scanned the room, and it seemed, if everyone had
served themselves, that I might be able to sneak into the pantry,
where I could sit on a stool off my feet for a couple of minutes
and have my meal.

I opened the back door to the pantry, hoping the cool air
would blow in. I was stirring my bowl of chili on my lap when I
heard someone clear their throat. I set the bowl on a shelf, and
back in the kitchen, one of the truck drivers stood with an
empty bowl. "Um-hmm, ma'am, may I have some more?"

Was he the one who didn't like chili? Was it him, or the man
who'd sat next to him when they'd arrived?

"Yes, of course."

When I finished my supper, I scraped my bowl clean and set
it by the sink, then gathered the other bowls. The same truck
driver who had just asked for another bowl came over from the
couch. "Ma'am, I'd like some more if you have any."

"I do." I scooped him a full bowl, and then gave him another
slice of corn bread. I stirred the pot since I'd need to keep some
chili hot for Roy.

Ted rose slowly and let out a sigh. He brought me his bowl
and rubbed his belly. "Ma'am, I'm gonna regret it because I had
too much, but that was the best meal I've had in months. I'll be
out for a walk. It looks like we might stay in our sleepers for the
night and come around tomorrow for breakfast if it's OK with
you?"

"Yes. Thanks for letting me know." I took Ted's bowl, which
looked like he might have even licked clean.

I let the dishes soak for a bit and scanned the pantry shelves
for breakfast ideas. It looked like there was plenty of flour for

biscuits. Now, what about bacon? I opened the freezer door to peer inside and pulled back some chunks of meat on top.

Suddenly, someone, or something, hit me with a powerful force, pushing my face into the open lid of the freezer. I assumed Roy had bumped into me, and I stood to place my hand on my head. The force of the shove shot a pain from my head and into my neck.

"Sheesh Roy, watch where you are going!" I opened my eyes and blinked.

No, it wasn't him. The room was empty.

Dazed by the hit to my head, my body tensed as it carried me to the doorway. I looked out and scanned the yard. Was there anything out of the ordinary? My heart pounded in my chest. Could I have imagined it? Did I slip on the floor I'd been meaning to sweep? Did I fall, or was it more of a shove? Why would someone push me?

My throat stung dry. I forced myself to go to the sink for some water The cold drink soothed the dryness. I grabbed a clean rag, ran it under the faucet, and placed it on my head. I took a deep breath and let out a sigh. Should I find Roy? Another few breaths and my heart would calm down. I couldn't stop working now. I needed to clean and organize the kitchen after supper.

I closed my eyes and let the cool rag soothe my pounding head. My heart nudged me to pray.

God, I don't know what to do.

I'd barely finished my prayer when the front door opened and in came Roy. "What's up with you? Are you OK?" He hurried to me.

"Were you just in the pantry? I think someone hit me from behind and slammed me into the freezer. I hit my head."

Roy stroked my shoulder and searched my head with his fingertips.

He walked into the pantry. "Nope. I've been in the garage.

Are you sure you didn't slip on the floor while you were ducking in the freezer to fish out food? I know I've caught myself on the floor before." He returned to my side, placing his hand on my back.

"I guess you might be right, but I am almost certain I felt someone or something hit me in my back."

"Not sure what to say, my love. I'll look out back."

He opened the door briefly, then closed it. "I don't see anything out of the ordinary." He walked over to the pot on the stove and helped himself to some chili. "Sit for a bit while I eat. Everything will be fine."

Fine? I hoped so.

Chapter 10

ROY'S TURN

THE NEXT MORNING, I PATTED THE BED NEXT TO ME. Roy's place was vacant. I squinted at the brilliant daylight that reflected off the clock on the dresser. Eight o'clock!

I scrambled to dress. How did I sleep in so late? Why hadn't I heard everyone moving around? The night before came reeling back to my mind, and so did my encounter with the suspicious stranger. Would he come back? Had he come back? I'd described the situation to Roy, whose snores told me he may or may not have heard me. I'd have to talk to him when he wasn't lying in bed.

I inched out of bed and moved to the mirror. Thankfully, my hair grew long this summer, and I devoted limited time for anything complicated in styling. My dark strands shone with lighter highlights from the intense Alaskan sun. I brushed it and gazed at my reflection.

A sleepy woman stared back at me, her eyes a dark brown with dull hues under them, warning me she lacked rest. Her face looked pale, considering it was the height of summer. I had plenty of time outdoors, but my early-morning fatigue must have drained the color from my face. I pinched my cheeks and quietly dressed before heading to the door. There wasn't a second to coddle myself. This was the liveliest part of the day!

As I continued down, there was little noise, just a steady clatter of forks clanging on plates and a cheerful tune echoing Roy's whistling. I shifted on the landing, inhaling the scent of sweet maple bacon. My stomach growled with a yearning to nibble some.

"Hi, Mommy!" Pam waved at me from the living room. She proudly leaned over the T.V. tray and raised a biscuit in greeting. "Daddy said we could eat in here!"

Of course he did. Dads are playful and fun—more willing to let something new slide. "Alright, be careful."

With a mouth full of bread, Rusty nearly upset his tray when he waved to me.

Roy stood proudly behind the kitchen counter with one of my aprons tied around his neck instead of his waist. It looked like a bib. I covered my mouth to catch my laugh, which almost seeped through my fingers. He raised the pot of coffee for me. "Good morning there, sunshine. Can I pour you a cup of joe? You need some since you snored like a freight train last night."

I smiled at him, then walked behind the counter and reached for a clean mug next to the stove. "Nah, listen here, little lady. You go on over there. I'll bring your breakfast and coffee. It's your day off!"

Could he be serious? I angled my head and studied his playful eyes, which glistened.

"Sit!" He pointed to a stool.

"Alright, if you say so." I searched around the room, saw the family who had stayed in the cabin lingering over their hot beverages, and their kids visiting with ours. "Did the truckers all leave?"

He leaned over the counter and quieted his voice. "One of

them asked for chili for breakfast. I obliged, of course. The rest of them ate their portion of biscuits and bacon, then rolled out. They left you a message." He leaned closer to me. "'Even though we may not have a black eye or need to check our eyes for pinholes, our convoy will certainly be back for some of your mud and lots of chili.'"

He darted his eyes right to left. "And *my* message for you is that you need to get a book on CB lingo so you can surprise them with your own coded reply when they return because, I guarantee you, they will be back." He snapped his fingers at the word back and gave me a playful pat on my shoulder.

"You know, you look good in an apron!" I sipped my black coffee and let my body relax on the stool.

He curtseyed.

A female voice came from the living room. "That boy makes a mean biscuit and bacon! You ought to have some." I turned to see a woman lift her plate and give me a thumbs up.

Roy leaned close to me and whispered. "She doesn't know I dropped hers on the floor. But it was the only one left, so I wiped it on my apron and put it back on the grill for a bit. What else do you do?" He shrugged as I cleared my throat.

"No way!" I tried to whisper my shock.

He placed a finger over his lips.

"Um-hmm." He lowered his voice. "You and the kids will leave for church here soon, so let me find you some of that bread my beautiful wife made, and I'll cook you a fried bird in a nest. My specialty."

I choked on my coffee and it burned my throat as it slid down. "For real?"

"No arguing from you." He pointed a wooden spoon at me. "Birgit called from Eagle, and she'll be back this afternoon." He spread his arms wide. "I can handle this."

I hoped so because this meant an unusual treat for me. I couldn't believe I had the day off!

"Deal." I sipped the hot coffee. Church would warm my soul, then I'd return to the embrace of Miner's Roadhouse.

Thank you, LORD!

THE PICKUP RUMBLED ALONG THE PAVEMENT ON THE way home from church in Tok. I beamed and tuned in to the kids singing in the rear seat. The day refreshed my spirit. Joy rose inside me, and I craved to burst out in song along with them, except I didn't know what they sang. I attempted to hum along. I hoped Roy's day was uneventful, and that he'd maybe have some left over food for us when we returned.

"It sounds like you've learned some new songs in Sunday school," I said.

"Mommy, I love singing to Jesus." I saw Pam in the rearview mirror, and she performed a dance with her stuffed bear cub.

"That's excellent because God loves it when you sing, but I don't always want to listen to you, Pam," said Rusty.

There it was! The pause was never too far between when sibling banter rose to the surface. No problem. A little nudge here and there kept things interesting.

We swung into Miner's entrance and saw multiple semis parked in the circle drive. *What now?*

"Wow, Mommy, look at all those trucks!"

I ushered the kids through the door into Miner's and along the counter sat six truck drivers. All of them were bent over their bowls with spoons in hand. Steam rose from their dishes.

Birgit poked around the corner of the pantry and beamed at us. "My family!" She hustled over to kneel and accept the kids' hugs. Then she stood up, smoothed her apron, and drew me in for one as well. "Sounds like you managed great, Lou! These men informed me Miner's is the talk of the ALCAN."

"Well, I did what you showed me. Welcome back! I assume your trip to Eagle went good."

Birgit moved behind the counter and brought out two brown paper bags. "It did, and I brought some treats home for the littles. Is it OK to give them a little something?"

Pam jumped in delight like a wee rabbit. I gave her a wide smile. "Yes, it's OK."

"Thank you, Aunt Birgit." They scurried to the living room.

I saw an opportunity to chat with Birgit alone and brushed her elbow. "Can we talk in the pantry?"

"Yes. You can show me your food tallies so I can arrange my next order."

Once inside, I paused with my back purposely to the kitchen so no one could overhear me. "Birgit, there was someone here last week who informed me he owns Miner's. He was gruff and rude, and I'm not sure what to make of it." I watched her for reassurance that the man had misled me.

Birgit let out a heavy sigh and clenched her jaw. Her eyes probed mine. Was she confused, or did she understand? Her pale hands stroked her braid.

"Lou, when my parents died, I wasn't yet eighteen, and I moved up north to live with my uncle. When I was older, I returned here. My parents passed Miner's on to me. I don't know who that man was, and I'm sorry that happened." She gave my arm a delicate squeeze.

"Could it have been your uncle? He looked old enough."

Birgit shook her head. "No, he wants nothing to do with this place. He said it was a hole, and I should burn it to the ground. Lots of things held me from coming back here, but I came anyhow. This is my dream, and now Miner's is alive again! You and Roy are the answer to my prayers!"

I believed Birgit. She never gave us any reason to doubt her.

"We're delighted to be here." I hugged her and snagged my apron, which dangled on a hook. "Now, put me to work!"

"Yes, best get her in the kitchen!" Roy appeared in the door-way, all smiles. "'Cause I hung up my apron, and I don't plan on putting it back on for a while." His teasing eyes danced as he planted an energetic kiss on my cheek.

Miner's was home! I grinned at Birgit and Roy. We fit in, making things work.

"Ma'am, uh, ma'am?" A man's voice interrupted.

I moved into the kitchen, and five of the truckers stood, money in hand to pay.

"Sorry. I'll take care of your payment over here," I said.

At the other end of the counter, I accepted their payments and looked into the living room to watch one lone driver in the corner. Why did he linger?

As I moved to soak the dishes, Roy arrived with some new ice to place in the cooler. When the other drivers left, the last truck driver rose from his chair and approached the counter slowly.

"If you have a moment, Roy, I need to explain some odd things I've noticed close to your place."

I altered the flow of the water, lowering the noise so I could overhear their conversation. I glanced over my shoulder at them.

"Sure, Joe. Want to sit in here or outside?"

"Let's go out."

Darn, I wanted to hear. I'd find out from Roy later.

"Lou, could you come here?"

Birgit stood in the pantry with a pad of paper that tallied the groceries. Her pencil was inserted into her bun, where it rested like a beehive on her head. "I can't locate some food I had brought from Fairbanks. Did you check off all the items you used with the extra customers we have experienced?"

I was careful about keeping excellent tabs on the supplies. A sense of order and structure was something I thrived on. "I've stayed on top of it. And I haven't ignored your system. I use it every time. We could ask Roy if he moved food when he was chef earlier today."

Did customers wander when I wasn't looking? Did Birgit suspect I took food? Because I didn't.

"Alright, I'll ask Roy," Birgit said. "When I unloaded, I may have recorded some numbers wrong. I'll confirm with my receipts. Thanks for your help, and I appreciate how you practice keeping records accurate and up to date. We're all new at this. I'm sure it's me who missed a step here. Oh, and I almost forgot—I picked something up for you as well. I'll go get it." Birgit put the clipboard back in its place in the pantry and slipped past me.

I went to the sink, scrubbed out the bowls and set them in the drying rack. I could hear the kids out back arguing about watering the garden. At least they argued about working. I gazed out the window and saw them dip buckets out of the rain barrel. Water sloshed out as Pam held the bucket up as high as she could. Did Rusty and Pam take food when I wasn't around? It would be a simple explanation since they wouldn't know to mark it off. I'd need to ask, and if it were true, put an end to it.

Birgit set a brown paper-wrapped package on the counter and clasped her hands. "Go ahead. Open it!"

Her delight was contagious. Her pure joy of life radiated in her words and actions. I admired her so much.

I unwrapped the light gift, and it revealed a shiny metal moon-shaped cutting edge attached to a short wooden handle. My face gave away my confusion. I didn't know what the implement might be.

Birgit giggled. "It's an Ulu knife. I doubt you've seen one before since they are unique to Alaska. We use them for almost everything." She held it in her hand and brushed the blade with a tender touch. "Some Alaskan natives out west use them to trim blocks of snow in the ice. I usually use mine for skinning and cleaning animals, but when I'm in Eagle, I use it for preparing salmon from the fish wheel. I hope you enjoy yours."

I placed the Ulu in my hand. It looked like a simple knife; I knew I held a veritable treasure. A gift of practical use and a jewel of wisdom and ingenuity. "Thank you Birgit, I'll look forward to using it."

A shattered scream broke from outside. I dropped the knife and ran out through the pantry. Birgit's steps followed mine.

I found Pam on her knees next to the fifty-five gallon rain-water barrel. I searched for the emergency. Where was the danger and pain I heard in her voice?

Pam was holding her foot and blood trickled out of the bottom of her shoe. "What happened?" I asked. "Let me look."

I took her shoe off even as a whimper shook her body.

Rusty, who was on his hands and knees next to me, held his gaze down. "She stepped on something sharp. Be careful, mom. I'll find it."

Birgit handed me a warm rag. "Now, now bear cubby, settle. We're here."

I gently untied the shoe with blood inside of it and held her foot in my hand. Birgit stroked Pam's hair and helped calm her as she sat in her arms. I pulled Pam's sock off and wiped her foot with the rag. She tried to ease her foot back, and I steadied it in my hand so she wouldn't fully pull herself away. "Hold tight. I need to see it."

"Mommy!" Pam's body trembled, and she stuttered out her words. "It...it...hurts."

"I know. I'm sorry. It looks like you might have stepped on a couple of nails. You have two holes in your foot."

"H-h-holes!" Pam screamed.

I shouldn't have used that word to describe the injury.

"You poked it." I held the rag on the wound and Birgit picked Pam up. "You'll be fine. Let's get it cleaned up, and you can sit on the couch and rest."

Roy came around the house. "What in the world?" he panted. He rushed to Pam and scooped her into his arms.

"Will you carry her in, Roy? She stepped on something sharp. A nail perhaps?" I looked over to Rusty, who searched the ground.

"I'm looking, Dad. I won't give up. I promise." Rusty kept his head down and patted the ground gently.

Roy's ashen face searched Pam's body thoroughly. Perhaps he recollected how frail her body had been when she was born, and how it left us helpless, praying for her to live.

"It's OK peanut. I've got you." He placed a gentle kiss on her head and carried her inside.

I stopped at the freezer in the pantry and found a popsicle. It might be a miracle maker. Roy set her on the couch, and Birgit placed a towel under Pam's foot. Her sobs eased now, and she wiped her tears on her shirtsleeve.

"Here." I handed her the frozen treat, and she gave me a stiffened smile. I sat next to her and pulled her close.

"I always go there…to get water. Why is it broken?"

Rusty ran in with a hand full of nails. "I found them in a pile, but I couldn't get the rest out of the ground!"

I looked at Roy, who stood over Pam and stroked her other hand. He gathered in Rusty as he came close.

"Good job, son! Hold my hand. This is a good time to pray about the sinister things that are creeping into our lives."

Chapter 11

Seasons Change

"I don't know what's going on here, but I don't like it! Not one bit." Roy set his coffee cup on the table, sat forward, and placed his elbows on his knees.

I'm not sure how to respond. I rubbed my forehead with my fingers and tried to force myself to think through the events of the last couple of weeks. How did it come to this? How do you put together pieces of a mystery without enough clues? The timer buzzed and drove me from my daydream.

I set my cup on the coffee table and turned off the timer. As I took the cinnamon rolls out of the oven, I inhaled the sweet aroma of the baked rolls, which reminded me of our first time at Miners. Perhaps today would be a new beginning.

Lord, help me to be hopeful.

Roy followed, placed his cup in the sink, and put an arm around my waist. "I'll be out in the garage, Lou. Shout if you need a hand, and send the kids out after they eat."

Today would mean more truckers traveling the highway, some with full loads and others headed south empty. They blessed our faithful crew with good numbers every day. I planned to carry the morning routine, and now that Birgit was back, she could tag team me in the afternoon. The day before, she'd suggested we take some family time and get away for the evening.

I blinked as I came out of my day dream, brushed the flour from my apron, and rolled up my sleeves. It was time to greet morning guests from the cabins with a hot breakfast at eight.

"THAT'S EASY!" ROY SHOOK THE TOWEL OUT WHILE WE sat at the bottom of the hill.

"I heard Julie talk about her kids begging to come play here. Now I see why! It's good clean fun....Well, maybe not clean. But fun." I picked up my towel as well. "OK, time to go. Roll down one more time!"

After supper, we'd decided to drive up the Taylor Highway and explore Fortymile country. We hadn't gone a quarter mile when Pam gasped in the back seat. She remembered the sand on both sides of the road from when we'd gone to the church's Bible camp, which was four miles up same road. She didn't have to twist Roy's arm for a second, he pulled right over and out jumped the kids. They'd run up the sandy hillside, then slid down over and over. Roy found some rocks near the bottom of the hill, and he'd placed them delicately in the sand, spelling out the kids' names.

Pam skidded down the hill. I'd assumed she'd favor her foot more, but she hurried to beat Rusty. At the bottom of the hill, his body moved faster than his feet, and he tumbled over.

He laughed and stood to brush himself off. "That's so much fun! Did you see how far I jumped?"

"You didn't jump, you fell!" Pam put her hands on her hips.

"Alrighty, let's make sure we get as much of the sand off as we can then head back to Miner's." I smoothed Pam's shirt and tousled her hair to remove any lingering sand.

"I'll tell Birgit I found an Alaskan treasure! She always tells me to hunt for it, and here it is!" Pam's eyes were wide as she spread her arms out as far as she could. She thrust herself forward as she made her claim on the sand dunes.

"Let's load up and head back." Roy held the door open on his side and swung his arm like a windmill in grandiose motion.

After we situated ourselves in the truck, Pam let out a big sigh. "I feel like I've always lived here in Alaska!"

"I know, Miner's is my home now too! Will Grandma and Grandpa visit us here?"

"Rusty, we will be back in another month or so, so they won't come here." I answered.

Silence filled the truck. I didn't want to hear it either. It was difficult to think of going home to Michigan. What would life look like if we stayed?

A number of vehicles filled the Miner's parking area when we arrived.

"Looks like Birgit needs a hand if you want to get the kids in the bath." I eyed Roy, then threw a glance at the kids.

"A baaaath!"

"Yes, Pam." I held the door open for the kids, and they ran in.

I froze when the stranger I'd met before leaned on the counter and listened to Birgit as she spoke.

I turned so I could quickly tell Roy, but he roared like a bear and chased the kids up the stairs.

Would my feet take me through the door? I forced them to move one step after another and plastered a smile on my face— my lips held tight. I walked across the kitchen and behind the stools, then entered on the other side, going right for the pantry. Birgit gave a quick wave midsentence as I passed. In the pantry, I put on my apron.

LORD, I don't know what to do.

His word entered my mind. "Be careful for nothing; but in every thing by prayer and supplication with thanksgiving let your requests be made known unto God." I reminded myself that the word careful meant anxious. I needed the reassurance.

OK, I'll rest in You.

I inhaled deeply as I crested the threshold and washed my hands at the sink.

The stranger rose from his seat and came my way. With each footstep, my heart beat faster.

"Well, hello there, lady." He stuck out a hand and I hesitated at the memory of his grip from the last visit. I wiped my hand on my apron and put my hand into his. I didn't look at him but at his massive hand that enveloped mine. His grip tightened, and he squeezed. I almost gasped at the intensity. I looked up at his dark, deep-set eyes.

"I'm Birgit's Uncle Floyd."

He sounded alarms within the inner core of my being. My heart beat rapidly, and I wanted so much to stand my ground.

Birgit's voice interrupted my downward spiral. "I'm so glad you came while my new family is here helping me breathe life into Miners for a season."

Is she blind to his eyes, which flashed when she spoke? Why did her words pierce him?

"Birgit, since I'm already down this way, I'm staying for a bit. The mining is slower than normal this year." He stood and smoothed his shirt, then placed his hat on his head. "So for you, my dear, I'll stick around." He scanned the room and looked from Birgit to me. "Why don't you get me some supper."

Is he asking? It sounded more like a command.

"Why don't you pull out one of those pies I've been hearing about." He continued to eye me with brazen gaze.

I turned to go to the freezer and hoped my burning neck wasn't visible because I was a Mamma Bear on alert. On second thought, I didn't care if anyone saw my neck. I would burst if prodded much more. I lifted the freezer lid and peered in, ready to take a pie from the top of the pile I'd put in Friday afternoon. Only there weren't any. Where could they have gone? I dug around since I may have moved them while looking for meat the other day, but I still didn't see any.

I went back into the kitchen and searched for Birgit but didn't see her. Nor did I see Floyd. Perfect. I left to find Roy.

In our room, he and the kids lay on our bed with their sticker books. The Polaroid pictures were laid out on the bed next to them. Apparently, they hadn't gotten in the bath yet.

After I dashed up the stairs, taking oxygen from my already racing heart, I tried to talk as calmly as I could. "Roy?"

LORD, I need You now.

"Can I talk to you please? In the hall?"

He had to see the panic on my face. Please, please.

"Yup. You two sit here. I'll be right back. Pick out one of your favorites to show me."

He held my shoulders and turned me into the hall, then carefully shut the door. "What is it? You look like you're going to tear the wallpaper right off the walls."

"Birgit's uncle is here. He's the one I told you about—the one who came before. He pretty much told me to make him supper and..." I tried to whisper but probably spoke too loud.

He put a finger to my lips. "Shh, say good night to the kids, go back, and I'll be right behind you."

One step at a time. Take your time. Slow down, and be calm. I formed one mantra after another in my mind, pacing the strength of emotion that burned inside me.

I was on a mission and went straight to the kitchen. Birgit had already made a delicious-smelling roast, and I searched for the leftovers to warm. My efforts to be quiet while I looked for clean pots were far from perfect, and I sent a clatter of echoes through Miner's. Roy's steps on the stairs announced his arrival, and he walked straight out the front door.

Maybe he'd find Birgit and her uncle? Would he find a way to expose the truth of this intruder? He was good with words. He talked to folks, and they often told him what was in their hearts. His sense of people and their true identities was something he easily assessed—a quality I admired.

After several minutes, the three of them came back inside laughing. I couldn't imagine what could possibly be so funny. My nerves were on edge, and I set the coffee pot onto the counter top abruptly. It cut the laughter like a knife through a watermelon, and the room went silent.

I turned to pull Floyd's food out of the oven and heard the voices quietly resume their chatter in the living room. Maybe I could find a reason to go upstairs away from everyone.

"Is it ready?" Floyd looked over at the kitchen toward me.

Birgit rose, came over and waved at her uncle. "You are such a bossy pants. I'll go get your food and coffee."

As Birgit lifted his plate, she leaned toward me. "He's always been the cranky type who tells his mining crew how to do their work. I guess, after a while, he assumes it's OK to act like that wherever he goes." She rolled her eyes. "I tried to help whip him into shape when I lived there. It sounds like I'll have to reign him in again. Thanks Lou." She carefully carried his food over to where he sat on the couch.

Maybe I'd misinterpreted his antics and gruff first impression. I averted my gaze from the group, went to the kettle, and filled it with water. The pain in the back of my throat drew me to make some tea to take upstairs while the kids bathed. Why was I so quick to judge?

I hadn't mentioned the missing pies to Birgit and went to the freezer to look again. Maybe something could be used as a replacement. I pulled items out and placed them back in again, confirming what my tally books already said. Items were missing, period!

The kettle whistled and drew me back into the kitchen. I poured my cup of hot water, ready to escape and take care of the kids. Roy would figure out the situation, and I trusted he'd fill me in.

"I couldn't find any pies, and I'm headed to give the kids their baths if they aren't already asleep." I carried my cup and didn't even look up for a response.

As I stepped onto the landing, Floyd rebuked my exit. "You owe me!"

I owed that grouchy man nothing. I was going to enjoy my kids and do my best to forget Uncle Floyd.

Chapter 12

REALITY

I GLANCED AT MY WATCH AS I LATHERED SOME lotion on my dry hands. It showed seven thirty. I leaned against the door and watched the kids giggle on the bed, absorbed in their own world. The pleasant summer-morning sun shone sharply onto the log walls, glistening gold and reminding me of the gift of a fresh newness brought with each day.

Thank YOU, Lord, Your mercies are new! My focus on Floyd was harsh last night, and I reacted negatively. Help today be different.

"Mommy, come and see the moose picture. Remember...the picture of his..." She couldn't finish the sentence. Her tiny frame curled onto the bed, and she laughed from her belly.

I smiled. "Time to start our day," I reminded her.

The kids coughed and sputtered from laughter and followed me out the door, ambling down the wooden staircase ahead of me.

They'd often sleep in, wandering sleepy-eyed into the kitchen in the late morning to ask for a biscuit or cinnamon roll.

Roy and I had visited last night about including them in our schedule.

Pam jumped off the step and slipped, letting out a scream as she slammed into the ground. I squatted to help her and lifted my head to scan the room. One young couple sat at the counter, and their bodies turned to the commotion at the steps. I smiled at them as I eased Pam up.

"What is all that ruckus?" I hadn't seen Floyd with his back to the grill flipping pancakes. He spun around and waved a spatula at Pam. "You need to slow down and be quiet."

Roy had assured me the night before that my experiences with my older brother tainted my view of Floyd. He encouraged me to give him a chance. His rough ways were prevalent enough, and we'd soften him. I wasn't so certain.

"Let's go." I signaled for them to follow me. "We'll go find Daddy before you eat."

Sheesh, what a grouch that man was! The kids didn't need to see me upset with him, especially in front of patrons. Also, if I lingered much longer, Pam was assured to give him a piece of her mind. I glanced back at the couple at the counter, and they continued to eat their food in silence.

"Mom, look at this mess!" Pam's voice of exacerbation drew my eyes to the messy shelves and white dusting all over the floor. "I bet—"

I put my hand over her little mouth and nudged her out the door ahead of me.

"Mommy! I was going to say the grouchy man made the big mess!"

"Which is why we left in a hurry. It wouldn't be nice to accuse him, Pam. Let's go find Daddy."

We found Roy whistling in the garage. I didn't want to linger long since I needed to help with the breakfast load.

"I'll be inside," I said. "Wait another half hour before you all come in to make sure everyone's done."

He nodded as he wiped his hand on a shop rag. "You two can be my attendants," he said to the children. "Put your work gloves on from the bench."

I remembered the mess in the pantry and shifted my steps to go through the front door instead. As I opened it, I held in a deep breath.

"It's about time you got here." Floyd waved the same spatula at me that he'd jerked at Pam earlier. It bounced as he flung it. "I don't know how we'll change your family schedule so you will be here ready when we need you. These people want coffee, and you didn't have it ready this morning. Birgit left in a hurry to get supplies in town, and left me foolin' around trying to help. Then you go off with your screaming kids, leaving me behind." He peered at me. "Well, don't just stand there. Light a fire under it!" He threw his arm in the air.

I moved to the other side of the counter as he mumbled under his breath and exited through the pantry.

"And clean up your mess in here!"

The quiet couple looked at their plates. The woman tucked her napkin under her plate, and a smile formed on her pale face. "We'll be going now. Do I pay you for our room as well?"

"Yes, ma'am. I'm sorry." I tilted my head toward the pantry.

The man rose from his stool and pushed it in. His eyes glanced from the stool to me. "No, ma'am. I'm sorry for you."

Yup, me too. Lord, I've been here before. I've been the object of rage. I need YOU!

EVEN THOUGH I WAS CERTAIN FLOYD HAD SOMEHOW made the mess, I cleaned the pantry from floor to ceiling. As I cleaned, I came across a small radio. When I plugged it in, I smiled to myself, listening to a hymn as it played crystal clear. I let the music work to bathe the wounds of the morning.

It was ten-thirty, and there were bound to be truckers rolling in anytime for their usual stop-and-go. I looked forward to their arrivals. They were so amiable and grateful, and a pleasant crew to please. As though my thoughts ushered them in, the front door opened, and five truckers crossed the threshold.

"Good morning, Lou!" Ted greeted me and removed his hat. He'd grown fond of a particular chair and strolled right to it. I moved to get him his coffee and serve him at his spot. The others sat at the counter and sipped the fresh water I poured into their glasses in expectation of their company.

"Good morning, Ted. What are you hauling today?" I tipped the pot to his mug and noticed his tired but smiling eyes.

"Ma'am, I'm back haulin' some grain from Delta to White-horse." He placed his feet on the ottoman and leaned back. He shut his eyes, then opened one. "And I need this cup of mud and a quick nap!"

I laughed out loud. "I'll leave you be."

Our usual banter brought me the satisfaction of a job well done and the knowledge that he saw Miner's Roadhouse as a home away from home.

Behind the counter, I filled mugs of hot coffee for the others and was carrying in the bowl of sugar cubes when a thundering voice startled me. The shock made my arms pulse, and the cubes flew in the air, landing on the floor.

"Who said you could listen to the radio? Turn that noise-maker off!" Floyd ripped the cord out of the outlet and slid it to the wall. His large hand kept moving as he raised it to point a finger at me, but it came down when he saw the men all in a row behind the counter.

Ted's voice carried from the living room. "We don't mind. Not one bit."

"It's not professional. Get these men some food, and get started with my lunch." Floyd spun on his boots and marched back into the pantry before anyone could argue.

Could I even argue?

All eyes were on me, and my face grew warmer.

Floyd's voice boomed to fill the brief silence and shot a tingle along my back. "Where are the pies I keep hearing about?"

The lid to the freezer slammed shut. His voice trailed off as he left out the back door and let it slam behind him.

My heart thumped hard in my chest. I wanted so much to take off my apron and run to Tok. Yes, I could sprint twenty-some miles with all the steam building and pumping through my blood. But I couldn't keep cleaning up these messes and dealing with the aftermath. Where was Birgit now? Surely, she'd be here soon to tame her uncle.

I looked past the men at the counter to see Ted in the living room. He shrugged and closed his eyes again. I had work to do and wanted to avoid the fury of Birgit's Uncle Floyd.

"Mom, is there a way I can help you?" Rusty peered at me from the stairs. His quiet steps had gone unnoticed. His eyes showed concern as he squinted.

What could I have him do that Floyd wouldn't misunderstand? Why did I have to consider it? "Want to pick some berries in the back? We'll make some muffins for tomorrow's breakfast. Take Pam with you. There's a bucket already on the picnic table out back." I smiled specifically to show him gentleness and reassure him that everything was OK.

"Yes, Mom." He hurried to obey and scurried out the door.

Ted's snoring must have lured the others to rest as well. Soon the three of them snored in harmony.

I smiled to myself. Only for a moment was there any peace, then Floyd came into the kitchen with his hat in his hand. He slammed his fist on the counter, and the truckers startled awake.

"This here is a business establishment, not a kindergarten classroom where we take our naps. You men can be on your way. Of course, after you pay your bill. Meanwhile, we are expecting other paying guests to arrive shortly," his pasted smile spoke vehemently.

Ted cleared his throat, rose from his seat and gave me a side hug. "Ma'am, I'll be back this evening after I return from White-horse. Don't worry, I'll pay my tab then."

"No." Floyd walked over to Ted and squinted his darkened eyes. "You'll pay us now, and if you come back, you can pay then. That's how it is here." His large right hand rested on the counter in a fist.

"Sir, I'll do as you please. I don't want Miss Lou to be in trouble. We have an agreement, and it works, but if it's what you'd like, we can all pay now." Ted slapped a large bill on the counter. "Ma'am, the change is your tip. Good day." Ted walked out the door and whistled himself a cheery tune.

God Bless Ted!

As each man passed, they nodded their heads to me and walked out. As the last man left, Birgit walked in, her arms full of brown paper bags.

"Let me help you." I grabbed a bag from her.

"Floyd!" She held one out for him to take.

He turned around like he hadn't heard a word and left out the pantry.

"Must be losing his hearing." Birgit let out a humph and set the bag on the counter. "I'll be back. Can you unpack those?" She walked out the door to her truck.

I unpacked the bags and opened the screen door for her. Roy carried the rest of her bags. I looked behind me and didn't see Floyd.

"I'll take care of these," said Roy.

He leaned into the back of the truck and placed the bags in a wagon next to him. I liked the idea. He knew how to make a job simpler. Roy pulled the wagon behind him and whistled his usual happy, light-hearted tune.

I let the screen door shut gently and helped unpack. Roy's

bronzed face glistened from the intense Alaskan sun. He wore the glow well, and all the work he'd done splitting wood had toned his muscular arms. The strength he'd gained in his early years of hard work was an asset at this job, which demanded heavy labor from day to day. He handed me an item that fell out of a bag and held my hand as it passed. I looked into his eyes.

"Is it going OK in here?" His soft and serious voice made me concerned that others may be listening.

I was grateful we'd decided last night on some code words we could use to communicate if my concerns escalated, but he'd seemed certain I wouldn't need them.

Pam's first puppy, which had died early on in an accident, was trouble from day one. We determined using the pup's name in a sentence could suggest trouble might be on the horizon. I coined a happen chance statement, hoping he would understand its meaning. "It's been a Slippery Doogin' of a morning, Roy!" I shook my head with my lips pursed. "You know, the same old thing."

Birgit passed by, holding a bag of oranges in her hand, and stopped to look at me. I guess she knew me well enough already to sense I was acting queer.

"Really now?" She smiled at me and then placed the oranges in the fridge.

Roy unloaded the wagon quietly and continued for the door. "Come on out, I have some things in the garage I found, and you might be able to use them in here." He gave me a wink and went out.

"Go on." Birgit spoke from behind the open fridge door.

"Be right back." I shut the door behind us and knew Birgit heard what wasn't said.

Roy stood near the back of the garage and rummaged through a toolbox. The metal echoed in the framed shelter. He turned around, holding a hammer in his hand that was smoothed across the handle. "So, what are you trying to tell me?"

It was time he knew how passionate I still felt about the situation. I pulled a step stool out from against the wall, took in a deep breath, and stared intently at my powerful man. I told him about my morning, not leaving anything out.

"I'll stay closer during the day. We need to let Birgit handle the conflict when she is there since it's her uncle. Keep the kids closer, and we will pray God will make it clear to us what to do." He pulled me in and held me close for a hug, the smell of fresh wood chips clinging to his shirt.

I was safe in his arms, the arms of a man who was now a devoted family man.

"DADDY, LOOK AT ALL THESE RASPBERRIES WE picked." Pam stood on a chair, reached into the sink, and pulled out a handful of red berries.

"I see them, peanut." Roy moved his arm from around my shoulder to the couch. "Good job. You and Rusty are good helpers."

I'd spent the afternoon on laundry and making pies. The kids picked berries, then helped Birgit. She was good at including them and teaching them along the way. There was a lull before supper and the arrival of overnight guests. It wasn't often we sat together rekindling the joy of simply being near one another. I savored Roy's closeness today after a rough morning.

"Dad, Birgit said today that soon we will have moose hunters stopping in on their way up the Taylor Highway. Isn't it neat?" Rusty walked from the kitchen up to Pam, then sat on the ottoman and faced Roy. "She said some guys even come from Juneau. She showed me on a map how far away it is. There must be some huge moose around here!" Rusty looked at Pam and pointed to the mount on the wall anchored above us. "Can you imagine Dad shooting a big bull like this one?"

"Sounds like a dream come true, Rusty! Maybe one day you'll get your turn." Roy removed his arm from around my shoulder and leaned on his knees with his elbows. He smiled at Rusty, who held a pretend rifle and shot at the moose frozen in time on the log wall.

"Honey, those are beautiful raspberries!" Birgit's voice filled the room as she walked in from the pantry, tied her apron around her waist, and approached Pam. She gave her a squeeze, then gathered her off the chair and set her on the counter. "Now, do you want to help me make these into some delicious muffins?"

Pam lifted her arms in the air "YES!"

I was so glad Birgit was going to help Pam. My feet ached, and it felt so good to stay seated.

"Get her off the counter. And why is everyone sitting around here?" Floyd's booming interrogation announced his arrival through the front door.

"She's fine, Uncle." Birgit looked at Floyd and pulled a bowl out from under the counter.

"I said get her off." He pointed at Birgit with an outstretched arm, then turned to look at us in the living room. "Isn't there something you need to do?" He directed his question at me, and I rose off of the couch.

Roy placed a hand on my shoulder and gently pushed me down.

"Her name is Lou, and you will show our family respect." Roy stood tall and walked to Floyd.

Floyd took a step forward. "Respect? It's your family who needs to respect me!" Floyd pushed a finger into his own chest. "I own Miner's Roadhouse! You work for me."

"Uncle Floyd, stop!" Birgit came over and stood between them. "Why are you talking nonsense?" She turned to face him.

"Birgit, I told you Miner's is yours, but I never signed it over to you."

Birgit gasped sharply and raised her hand to her mouth. "Uncle Floyd, you didn't?" She pulled her apron to her chest.

"I always thought that this place was a foolish dream of your parents and that you were crazy to get it going. I see now though that it's bringing you some money, and now it's time for me to help you do it right."

"Right? You come in here and bark orders." Roy remained in place and stood his ground. "Somehow that makes it all good?"

"Listen here, little man." Floyd thrust his chest out. "You'll do what I say, and I say get to work. You won't be telling me what's right from wrong."

Pam jumped off the counter, ran to Roy and hugged his leg. He put his hand on her head, then raised his other hand at Floyd. "If you're going to tell me what to do, then we're leaving."

"You can't leave." Floyd took a step closer to Roy.

"There have been enough disconcerting events that have pushed us in this direction. We can only wonder if it's you that's steered us. You can't force us to stay. We'll leave in the morning."

Roy's words pelted like hail from a summer tornado. The sudden and chilling sensation washed over me. Our adventure was over.

Birgit's sobs broke the chill of Roy's statement. I rose to give her a hug. Rusty joined me, and so did Pam. Roy came over and put his arm on Birgit's shoulder. "I'm sorry, Birgit."

Together, we embraced Birgit, who shook from her cries.

"You'll be here in the morning." Floyd's attempt to command us fell on deaf ears as we stood and held Birgit.

Dear Lord, is this how it ends?

Poor Birgit!

Help us all, LORD!

Chapter 13

BACK TO MICHIGAN

ROY'S DELICATE TOUCH WOKE ME UP, AND I PULLED myself from Pam's grip on my head. I scooted to the edge of the bed and stood to face my husband. I tried to study his face for a sign of how he was. He placed a finger to my lips, leaned over and whispered in my ear. "Come over to the chair."

He held my hand as he sat, and he pulled me into his lap. He turned my chin lightly to him. "Lou, I know this is the best and safest thing for us to do. I should have tuned in to your clues earlier because your gut instincts were correct."

I leaned my head against his chest and inhaled his Old Spice scent, which sent me swirling back to the first time we'd met. A smile formed on my lips. Here we were with two kids curled in our bed, headed for the highway to the unknown. I yearned to let God's calm presence bring peace to this turbulent season we found ourselves in.

"I love you," I said.

He smoothed my hair with his hand. "Love you too, very

much. Let's get everything ready to go. We've a long day ahead of us."

Yes, a day with lots of tears and questions from the kids. I detested having to rip them away from the fairy-tale life we dove into here at Miner's. A knot formed in my stomach from a familiar ache, the emptiness of losing something I'd grown to love.

"Roy, can you pray for us?"

"Let's get the kids up first. It'll be good for them to hear our prayers for God's guidance and peace."

AS WE STEPPED DOWN THE STAIRS OF MINER'S roadhouse, I could smell coffee and the distinct aroma of burnt toast. I moved from the landing and peeked into the kitchen. A row of truckers leaned over the counter and picked at their food. We each held our own bag and set them by the door. I froze in place. *Where do I turn, and what do I do?* The last thing I wanted was to have an encounter with Floyd and leave in an emotional wrestling match.

A familiar voice spoke. "Ma'am, where are you goin'?" Ted rose from his stool at the end of the long counter and wiped his mouth with his napkin. He walked to us slowly, gazed at the bags, then back at us.

Birgit and her Uncle faced the grill.

Roy spoke before I could and stepped to Ted, his hand outstretched for a handshake. "Headed back to Michigan."

"You love it here. There must be something you aren't sayin'." He looked directly at me, his eyes wide and searching.

Like a volcano with a fierce explosion, Floyd erupted from his post at the grill with a fire-red face and glared at us.

"Ted, Miner's is owned and now operated by Floyd. We're leaving." Roy set his hat on his head.

My eyes stung with tears, and a lump formed in the back of my throat. I longed to reach out to Birgit and pry her out from under her Uncle's pressing force. I knew how suffocating captivity was.

"If you leave, we will too." Ted dug in his front pocket, pulled out some cash and set it on the counter. "Miss Birgit, I'm sorry for your loss, and for the fact that I won't be back. Good day to you, ma'am." Ted nodded in her direction, and Birgit didn't look up from what busied her.

Ted kneeled down. The kids pulled away from my arms and reached for his embrace. He was a friend to us all.

The other truckers rose from their seats and followed Ted's lead, each taking money out of their wallets and placing it on the counter.

As I shook the truckers' hands, I envied their family bond—they shared the experience of traveling Alaska and the ALCAN. They were the backbone for transferring supplies to many businesses like Miner's, and they stood by each other.

Floyd cleared his throat and let out a grunt. He grew from red to purple, cursed beneath his breath, and stomped out the back.

Birgit turned and ran to us, tears streaming across her face. "I love you all, and goodbye!"

Pam cried and Rusty sniffed.

Birgit wiped her eyes with her apron and formed a smile. "I'll always be so grateful for my family. Send me a postcard, Rusty!"

How could we leave? But we couldn't stay. I drew in a deep breath and placed my hands on the kids. "Goodbye, Birgit."

Roy put his hand on the small of my back and ushered us out the door of Miner's Roadhouse.

We stepped into the warm August morning. The truckers were all in their trucks with their engines running.

We climbed in our pickup and pulled out of the Miner's parking lot, and the convoy of rigs followed.

Goodbye, Miner's.
LORD, what now?

Chapter 14

IDEAS

I LONGED TO DO MORE TO SAVE THE TAN PUPPY THAT lay limp in Rusty's folded arms. We'd been up all night, cuddling little Boo, who shivered and whimpered. It broke my heart to watch the pup suffer, and I prayed he would survive. The kids had coined the dog's name when we discovered him all curled up next to our garage on our return home from Alaska a couple of weeks before. We tried to approach him, and he acted skittish, playing hide-and-seek as we looked for him.

Eventually, he grew to trust us. Then he adopted us as his family, and we were happy to take him in. His awkward walk, where his front legs moved quicker than his back ones, left us all roaring with laughter. We needed to laugh and find something to love. I thanked God for our Boo, who helped fill a hole in my heart.

Startled by Rusty's abrupt movement on the couch as he awoke, tiny Boo opened his deep-brown eyes, gazed at Rusty, and whined so quietly I strained to hear. I brushed my hand on his head all around his face, shushing him, hoping to assure him and myself that he'd be OK. On the floor, I leaned over Rusty, who aroused and rubbed his eyes.

A knock at the door surprised me, and I moved to peer out the peephole. Roy was out hunting with his dad, and I was doing my best to hold myself together at home with the kids. Who would come over so early in the morning? I turned on the porch light. Jim stood outside. I unlatched the lock and opened the door.

"Good morning, Jim. Come in." He stepped inside and went to the couch.

"Good morning, Lou."

He kneeled next to Rusty to pet Boo, then pulled out a Tupperware container, popping the lid. He waved the Tupperware top and a delicate trace of steam ascended from it. "I did some reading and have some special food for Boo." He looked at me smiling. "It's chicken and rice, isn't it nice?" He snickered at his own rhyme. "Have a spoon I can use?"

I went to the kitchen to snag a spoon and a rag. How did we know Boo would hold it down? How kind of Jim. How early did he get up to cook?

"I know what you're thinking." He reached up and took the spoon from my hand and pulled Boo from Rusty's arms to cradle Boo in his own. "Faith made the soup, and I picked it up. She'll make one wonderful wife! Um-hmm, she made the shredded chicken and found some bone broth to cook the rice in. Boo won't be able to resist. It's making my stomach growl smelling it."

"Mommy, how's Boo?" Pam's high-pitched morning voice trailed down the hall. She came near the living room and rubbed her eyes. "Hi Pastor Jim! Why are you here?" She glanced over at Rusty on the couch and sat next to him, both of them perched on the edge.

I watched Jim nurse the dog with his gentle touch, and the tiniest bit of thick soup on the tip of the spoon.

"Pastor Jim? Are you a dog doctor too?" Pam asked.

Jim laughed out loud and Boo shivered. "No, Little Pam, I'm not, but God is, and the soup might be what helps. Maybe at the end of today he'll run around the living room and nip at your shirt."

Boo sniffed at the spoon while his eyes batted open and shut. His small tongue lapped at the soup.

"Ah, there you go, little buddy." Jim stroked Boo's head with his other hand while Boo nestled on his lap.

"It's Boo, not Buddy." Pam's correction didn't surprise me. I smiled at her when she looked at me, her shoulders straightened. "I named him."

"I'll do my best to remember." Jim gave Pam a friendly wink and praised the dog's efforts. "Good boy, Boo. Have some more." Jim looked at the kids. "Do you know what kind of dog you have here Rusty?"

"We aren't sure. Dad says he's a lab mix of some sort, but I guess we'll see." Right now, we think he's maybe eight weeks old."

Rusty helped with Boo and around the house. His time at Miner's had added to his innate sense of responsibility.

A gentle knock on the door grabbed my attention. I opened it for Faith, who energized the room as she entered.

"Hi, I came to see Boo. Oh, he's the cutest little dog!" She cupped his face in her hands. "Oh hi, Jim." She stood next to him and brushed her shoulder with his. "Can I hold him?"

Jim tenderly set Boo in her arms as she took a seat on the couch.

"Come sit with me, Pam," Faith said, "and tell me something I haven't heard about your trip to Alaska."

Those two could talk all day to each other.

Jim walked to the kitchen and helped himself to some coffee on the stove.

It was good to be home and be with friends. I moved to the

kitchen and sat at the table. I smoothed my hand along the top of it, familiar with every nick and scratch. It had heard many deep and long conversations.

Rusty came over and sat next to me, his elbows on the table, and looked over at Jim. "Uncle Jim? My teacher told me there is school after school. Did you know that?"

I wasn't sure where the question came from. I raised my eyebrows, curious to see where this would lead.

Jim pulled a chair and grinned at Rusty, then turned the chair around, straddled it, and set his coffee on the table. "Not sure what you mean there."

"My teacher told me that after school you can go to more schools and learn to be a teacher or doctor. I didn't know there's more school!" Rusty ran his hands through his brown hair. "It hit me when we came home: I'm a long way from done. I want to finish fast, Uncle Jim, so I can hunt all the time, and now it turns out there's even more school." He shook his head and looked over to me. "Mom, did you do school after school?"

"Nope." I disliked school and understood his frustration.

"I went to school after school, and it's where I learned about being a pastor. Rusty, when it's something you love, school can be fun. Don't worry, there'll be lots of time to find out what you want to learn about. Maybe you'll find some school that teaches about hunting and fishing. Or maybe you'll become a game warden and catch all those poachers!"

Rusty laughed out loud and set a hand on the table. "Sounds like fun school to me!"

Pam and Faith giggled about something in the living room. Oh boy, those two were like peas in a pod! Little Boo let out the tiniest bark. The room fell silent.

"He told us to talk quieter, Pam. I guess we better listen. Sorry

Little Boo. Here is some more soup. He likes it, Pam. Look at him, licking his lips..." Faith took over and nursed the dog. My hope was that no matter who held him, he felt loved and would fight to keep going.

The door swung open and in came Roy, his gun slung over his shoulder. He removed his hat and hung it on the hook by the door. "Sounds like a party's going on in here!"

I left my seat and went over to give him a kiss hello. "You're back early!"

"I hope it's OK." He gave me another kiss and then looked to hug Pam, who came over, giggled and hugged his leg. "Hey, peanut! This certainly is an early-morning crew we have here!"

"Dad, it's Boo. He's been sick." Rusty rose from the table and stroked Boo on the head. "He's been eating some soup Miss Faith made. He's going to be OK. I asked God to help him."

Roy leaned over and gazed at the dog, then back at Rusty. He gave him a shoulder rub, then came and sat down.

I handed him a cup of hot coffee. "Get a deer?"

"Dad did. He wants us to come and help process the meat later." Roy looked over at Jim, who sipped his coffee. "What's new with you, Jim?"

"Not much. I admit I'm a little jealous that you went on a hunt so early this year. I've been waiting for my brother to come so we can go together. I have a question for you though."

"Oh, yah?" Roy sipped his coffee and smiled at Jim. It hadn't even been a year since our friendship with him had begun, and now it felt like we'd known him for years.

"I pray for you a lot." Jim rose from his chair and turned it back around. "Has God impressed you with anything lately? Because I have some ideas for you."

"Sounds dangerous, Jim." Roy's way of turning a conversation casual was a gift that still amazed me.

What was this all about?

"Have you considered Bible school?"

Jim's inquiry shocked me. Where was Bible school? What would it mean for the rest of us if Roy was in school?

"I have." Roy leaned on the table and looked directly at Jim.

Rusty looked up from the leatherwork he'd brought to the table. "It sounds like another school-after-school idea. Bible school. Maybe I'll go one day, too!"

I spun my wedding ring on my finger. More changes and uncertainty. Were we supposed to open ourselves up for more after all we'd endured already?

"There's a school here close by, but I did more looking and found one in Alaska you might consider since you grew to love the lifestyle up there so much."

Alaska? Would we go back? I looked at the clock. When should I make some breakfast? My upset stomach cautioned me to wait; however, my dry mouth longed for some of our cold well water. I raised myself from my chair and went for a glass.

"Where in Alaska?"

"In Glennallen. When I looked at a map, it seemed close to where you were in Tok. Well, at least in the same general area. Did you want me to call them and ask more about it? I have some general questions, and it'd be good to learn their stance on various doctrines."

"Yes, that'd be good." Roy looked at me. "Can I have more coffee?"

I went to the stove, carried the pot and steadied myself with the counter. *LORD, really? You think I can handle more?*

My grace is sufficient...

Another verse we'd learned. Spending some time in prayer with the journal, like Judy once suggested, popped into my mind. I'd need it to write the cries of my heart.

Boo's faint bark startled me. I peeked into the living room as I poured Roy's coffee. The pup's tail wagged, and his head perked up as he looked around.

Aw, thank you, LORD!

"Mommy, Mommy, Boo is better! Jesus helped him!" Pam bounded off the couch and ran to give me a hug.

"Yes. He must like Aunt Faith's soup!"

"Maybe, but she's right. It's Jesus!" Faith gave Pam a high five.

"Looks like Little Boo might need to get good and strong if he's going to be a tough Alaskan dog!"

Jim's comment spun my mind downward. In my mind, we had arrived home to stay. I chewed on the inside of my cheek and caught myself. When everyone left, I'd pull Roy aside and ask more about his impressions. Where he saw us a year from now?

"Hey, daydreamer, come on over and sit with us girls." Faith drew me in, and I was glad for the reminder to be present. She patted the seat next to her and smiled widely at me. Her blonde hair fell to her shoulders, and she tossed it back with her hand. Her friendship was a gift I treasured. I'd missed her while I was away.

"Sure, if I can have a turn with Boo!" I scooped him up and petted his soft silky fur. I stroked his back, and his warmth in my hand drew me to continue to plead for him to live. I couldn't stand to have something ripped away so soon like we had been from Miner's. Saying goodbye was so horribly hard.

Chapter 15

TEARS

THAT NIGHT, ROY SPOKE WITH EXCITEMENT IN HIS voice. "Remember when Rusty called Norvell 'doorbell' because he thought it's what we said? Kids! He's growing up so fast, talking about being a game warden, then going to Bible school. I'll take him hunting with me next time. He's mature enough. I'll buy him his own rifle soon."

We lay in bed and visited before turning off the light. I was irritated at Roy's chitchat. Could our conversation be about my expectations? I supposed it'd be different when we returned, and now we were entertaining Bible school. What an outrageous thought, living in Alaska!

I rolled over to face him. He was on his back, staring at the ceiling. Ever since we'd arrived home, I'd tossed and turned, reliving those last days at Miner's. I even broke into a sweat when I remembered Floyd's fire-burning stares. Did Birgit still endure his oppressive ways? My heart grew heavy, and I drew the covers off my shoulders.

"Roy, when I was young, I didn't dream like our kids do.

They imagine what they want to be when they grow up." As a kid, I couldn't picture life any different from what it was. The same was true now. "You're talking of Bible school in Alaska. Should we be half-serious? I don't know what to think." Had I ever spewed out my gut feelings before? I couldn't hold it in. I wiped a tear from my eye onto my pillowcase.

He twisted over, faced me, and stroked my cheek with his fingertip. "I remember when you dreamed about the future. It was a life with me. You said so in your letters, like when I was in the Army. Look around the room. We designed this home and built it together. You can dream Lou. Let God help you."

Maybe I didn't want to. All I wanted was for things to remain the same.

"Here, I'll start." He held out his hand with his pointer finger up. "One, we move to Alaska—dreams come true." He raised his middle finger next to his pointer. "Two, I go to Bible school surrounded by Christians—sounds like heaven to me." His ring finger came next to the others. "Three, we have a fresh start."

My mind lingered on the image of heaven on earth. Was it wonderful living near so many like-minded people? The idea rose in me and flooded me with warmth.

"So? What do you think?" He gave my side a gentle poke. "How about we pray about it? Ask God for a clear direction."

"We prayed about Miner's and look where it left us! How does it all work?" I grimaced and turned my mouth in a twist.

"Oh, don't show me that face. You might scare me!"

His teasing and light-hearted approach ground on my last nerve. I brushed away another tear. "I'm serious. How do I know to trust God in this?"

"Remember the verse from Proverbs that Jim shared and asked us to memorize? Didn't it say trust the Lord with all your heart and not to lean on your own thoughts? Let's pray and take it to the LORD."

I knew the verse. I'd memorized it right away. Part of me didn't want to pray—to trust with my whole heart. I wasn't good at that.

He pulled the covers over my shoulders and tucked them in. "We'll be fine, Lou. God's with us all the way."

All the way. Give it all. Trust Him with all... You must show me, LORD.

"SELL THE HOUSE! IT'S WHAT HE SAID." I STOOD WITH my hands on my hips and stared at Faith, who had stopped by early in the afternoon.

She moved closer and rested her hand on the wooden Adirondack chair next to the grass.

"I'm sorry, Lou. It makes sense to me." She sat on the chair, leaned over, and rested her elbows on her knees.

I pulled the other chair over and positioned it across from her. "I figured we'd go to Bible school and come back. Not sell it all and leave forever." I threw my arm in the air and lowered my head. I tried to keep in the tears that stung my eyes.

"Lou." Faith held my hand in hers. "Alaska sounds like an excellent fit for your family. The experiences at Miner's—even as difficult as it was when it ended—remember you told me how much you enjoyed your life there! Cling to those blessings and let them be your focus. God has you in the palm of His hand. Similar to how my hand holds yours now. Except his is much bigger." Faith let out a slight giggle and leaned in, looking deep into my eyes.

"I know, but we're just starting here...finding our part in the church. You and Jim are like family to us."

We let each other's hands go, and she gave me a tissue.

"And we will always be here for you. The family of God is everywhere! Even in Alaska." Her teasing voice raised a pitch.

I wiped my eyes, but the tears streamed. My shoulders shook. "Faith, I don't know how I can do this. It hurts so much."

She hugged me and whispered, "I'll keep praying for you."

Her efforts were admirable. I yearned to have the desire to agree. This idea of moving spun my world out of control, and I wanted to slow down so I'd find my way.

Oh GOD, I desire Your peace.

Boo's licks on my toes surprised me, and I opened my eyes. The tickle brought a smile to my lips. "Stop, Boo." I gave him a gentle push with my hand, but he came back to my feet and continued.

"He tastes the salt from your tears! That's so sweet!" Faith scooped him up. "Oh, Boo, are you the little angel Lou needs? I know you're no angel, but she needs you." She held him out for me to take. "Here."

I took Boo from her. He sniffed my face. When he went to lick me, I pulled him back. I let myself relax, then sensed his puppy excitement in the wag of his tail and his jittery movements. After inhaling deeply, I sighed. I forced a smile and gazed into his brown eyes. "I suppose God knew we needed you, Boo. What do you think about Alaska?"

His tail wagged, and he let out a little bark.

"Yah, me too." I looked over at Faith. "I don't know." I turned my head to look down the driveway. "I hear the kids getting off the bus. Guess I better get myself together."

I stood to touch Faith's shoulder. She raised herself up and gave me a hug all in one motion.

"Lou, you've been an encouragement to me since I came here. I want to return the friendship. Let me know how I can help."

"I will."

I looked at the driveway, watching Rusty walk while Pam skipped along. Her skip turned into a run.

"Aunt Faith!" Pam's explosive greeting brought a smile to my face. I needed joy like Faith had.

She prepared for Pam's running hug, kneeling at her level. Pam squeezed Faith's neck. "Did you see how Boo runs around?"

"Yes, I sure did! You must take good care of him!"

"She does." I smoothed Pam's hair and reached for the lunch box in her outstretched hand.

Rusty continued to saunter along the driveway and called for Boo.

"Mommy, I have the best news. My teacher says she wants to buy our place! Isn't it wonderful! I told her we're moving. She said she's heard what an amazing house Daddy built and gave me this." Pam held out a folded piece of white paper.

I took the note and opened it to see her teacher's name and number. I put it in my pocket and hoped I might forget to pull it out when Roy came home. No, there were no secrets, and Pam would tell him. It was all too fast! Much quicker than I wanted.

"Hi, Mom, can I have a snack?" Rusty held Boo in his arms and let the dog gnaw on his finger. "We need to find a chew toy for him." His cheerful laugh spread a smile across his face.

"Oh, that reminds me. I brought you all cookies." Faith went to her car and pulled out a metal tin from the back seat. "They are no-bakes. I hope you like those kind."

"Mm, sure do." Pam held Faith's arm. "Let me show you where you can put those." The two of them skipped to the open garage door, and Rusty followed.

I sauntered along. Did I have to leave this normal life behind? My steps slowed, and I looked around. I loved the home we built, the yard we planted, the large trees that surrounded our acreage. If we left now, how long until we had our own home again? I didn't want another unsettled move from place to place like we'd done when we were building.

A breeze moved through the trees, and the wind brushed my

face. A chill made me shiver, and I crossed my arms in front of me. As I walked across the garage, I could hear the kids and Faith converse above me.

I took hold of a ceramic pot on the workbench. I touched it and rubbed my fingertips along the top of it. My mom had given it to me for our wedding with a plant in it. Would it travel the thousands of miles with me? We wouldn't just be leaving our home, but our dear friends and everything I'd ever known.

I sat on the stool and glanced around the garage. Roy and I had poured the cement for the floor while Pam played in the wheelbarrow and Rusty kept himself busy pounding screwdrivers into the dirt. There were memories everywhere I looked. They were in our home, the town, and the stores. The familiar everyday view would never be the same again.

Selling the house would mean not turning back and learning to call Alaska home. How long until I'd have fresh memories to look back on?

Alaska, with its unique culture and way of living, daunted me. Birgit showed me how the women of Alaska were a caliber beyond what I saw myself capable of. How could I face long winters with confidence? Or even know how to prepare?

I rubbed my eyes, then set my head on the workbench.

We were moving to Alaska.

Chapter 16

GOOD SAMARITAN

ROY TURNED THE RADIO UP AS WE DROVE NORTH UP
the highway in southern Alberta. I looked in the rearview mirror
and saw the landscape disappear behind us. I held my hand to
my dizzy head. It was our fourth day on the road, and I went
without any breakfast. Now all I wanted to do was be alone. I
doubted the move immensely.

The music to John Denver's tune "Take Me Home Country
Roads" slowly rose in volume, and the lyrics hit me like a sledge
hammer. Roy sung along and turned the music up even louder.
The kids joined in.

I stared out the frosty window and watched the snow-
covered fields zip past.

I pulled my coat up to my chin and closed my eyes. Perhaps I
could nap and time would go faster.

Earlier this week, at our last church service in Michigan, the
congregation sang a closing song: "Follow On." The hymn, unfa-
miliar to me, resonated in my heart, and I'd jotted down the

lyrics. I pulled out my travel bag to open the yellow pad of paper.

DOWN IN THE VALLEY WITH MY SAVIOUR I WOULD GO,
  Where the flowers are blooming and the sweet waters flow;
  Everywhere he leads me I would follow, follow on,
  Walking in his footsteps till the crown be won.

REFRAIN:
  Follow, follow, I will follow Jesus,
  Anywhere, everywhere, I will follow on;
  Follow, follow, I will follow Jesus,
  Everywhere he leads me I will follow on.

2 DOWN IN THE VALLEY WITH MY SAVIOUR I WOULD GO,
  Where the storms are sweeping and the dark waters flow;
  With his hand to lead me I will never, never fear;
  Dangers cannot fright me if my Lord is near.

3 DOWN IN THE VALLEY, OR UPON THE MOUNTAIN steep,
  Close beside my Saviour would my soul ever keep;
  He will lead me safely in the path that he has trod,
  Up to where they gather on the hills of God.

OH, HOW I LONGED TO ETCH THIS TRUTH FOR MY aching war-torn heart. *Follow, follow, follow...*I didn't want to follow this road, and I didn't want to sulk either. How could I weather the rumble of the storm inside me and still be kind and compassionate to my family who had joyfully surrendered their life in Michigan with excitement, then forged on?

The country music station played a new song, and Roy turned the stereo down. Windshield wipers hurried across the window to clear the splattered, sloshy mixture of rain and snow.

"Hey, Mommy, soon we will live in Alaska! What did you say the town is again? Will I have friends? Do you know where we will stay?"

Here were the rapid-fire questions I'd anticipated.

Without any warning, an explosion shook the whole vehicle. The deafening noise came from the camper. I clasped my ears and quickly looked to the back seat to see how the kids were. Their hands cupped their ears, and they both crouched over their lap as though, taking cover from debris.

"No!" Roy slapped the steering wheel with the palm of his hand. "One of the propane bottles exploded. I'll have to find somewhere to pull over." He maneuvered into the right lane and then slowed the truck. "I knew the guy filled them too full."

My heart raced wildly, I crossed my arms across myself to calm the shivers running up and down my arms.

"Daddy, Daddy, what about Boo?" Pam's voice screamed almost as loud as the explosion.

"There's an exit" I pointed a short distance ahead, and we were able to pull into a rest area.

Roy turned the truck off and signaled for me to follow. "Let's check on Boo and the camper."

I jumped out of my door as he climbed out of his, and we both dashed to the camper door.

As Roy opened it he looked at me. "Be prepared for the worst, Lou. Boo might not be OK."

I clasped my hand to my mouth and held onto the side of the truck. *Oh, LORD, let him be OK.*

In one swift movement, Roy opened the door and Boo

jumped into his arms, trembling. The poor puppy shook violently, and his eyes shifted from side to side.

"Oh poor, Boo, come here!" I held him tight so he'd know he was safe. "Dear Lord, thank goodness he is OK."

I stroked Boo, hoping to calm him and myself simultaneously.

"I'll look around in the camper. Get in the truck with him. I don't think he'll want to be back here for a long time. Especially not by himself."

I carried Boo tucked in close to me through the slushy mess. Already the wet, icy chill of snow soaked through my sweater. I opened the door, and the kids took him into the back.

Pam doused Boo with affectionate kisses and reassured him. "My poor baby, were you scared? It's OK, it's OK."

I rubbed my hands together and tried to warm them. How had the weather turned so quickly? Earlier in the morning, when we'd stopped to fill the propane tanks outside of Calgary, a woman told us the chinooks were common east of the Rocky Mountains. Wouldn't a warm wind mean less snow? It didn't seem possible for a bright sunny morning to turn to a dark snowy afternoon with such rapid force.

Rusty leaned forward on the seat. "Mom, is everything OK?"

From the rearview mirror, I could see Roy push on the camper window. What was going on?

"Your Dad knows what to do Rusty."

Roy opened his door. "Phew! Is it ever wet out there! How's the pup?" He reached back over the seat and gave Boo a head rub. "Poor little guy had quite the fright. The windows in the camper were already open a little, so it helped lessen the blow. I'm so glad everyone is OK."

He rubbed his arms with his hands, removed his hat, and set it on the middle console. Next, he rubbed his hands on his pant legs and fumbled around. He touched the key in the ignition.

"Ha, there it is. Let's get rolling and try to get out of this weather a bit."

As Roy went to put the vehicle into gear, another truck pulled in toward us with the driver's window facing Roy's.

Roy rolled down his window and the cool air rushed in.

"Everything OK?" A gray-haired man with a green ball cap on that read 'John Deere' smiled to us. "Folks don't usually pull in here since there isn't a restroom. I wanted to make sure you don't need anything."

"Thanks. A propane bottle blew up in the camper, but we're OK. It scared the dog real bad." Roy pointed to the back seat.

"Any damage to your camper?" He turned his pickup off and leaned out the window.

"My roof might have been blown up about half an inch, but we're good." Roy looked at me and smiled.

Was it a courtesy smile intended reassure himself as much as me?

"Why don't you follow me? I have a farm close with a large shop. You can pull in out of the weather and take a closer look. I see you have a Michigan plate, so you're likely far from home." The stranger smiled. "I won't take no for an answer." He rolled up his window and slowly pulled his truck forward.

"Well, thank you, Lord. He sent us help before we asked." Roy looked over to me, then took my hand and gave it a gentle squeeze.

We trailed behind the blue pickup on the highway to the next exit. The farms were scattered on both sides of the road. I couldn't even remember the last town we'd passed.

"Dad, will we be able to still use the camper?" Rusty's voice tensed.

We turned into a long driveway on the right to a ranch-style home. The silos towered behind the house, and to the left, stood a large metal building I assumed was the shop the man had referred to.

"Look, Mom, there are some sheep!" Pam pointed past my face to a gated fence where some sheep gathered.

The good Samaritan stopped his truck outside the shop and hopped out. He quickly walked over and opened Roy's door. "I'll go around back to open the shop. Looks like you have a crew in here." He smiled at us and gave me a nod. "Once we get in, your wife and kids can come over to the house. My wife is home. She'll be so happy to see that you all get dry and have some warm food if you need it."

Though I was hesitant of his offer and about to protest, Pam shouted out from behind me. "I'm so hungry I could eat a bear!"

"You could not!" Rusty nudged her with his elbow. "You are only hungry because someone talked about food."

"I should check this trailer better before we travel another two thousand miles." We pulled into the open garage bay, and Roy turned the truck off.

Our family ambled out of the truck and watched the farmer go over to the wall near the door. He picked up the phone.

"Yah Ma, I have some visitors for you. Yup, they were on the highway. OK, sure thing. Bye, hun." He set the receiver back on its mount and waved us over.

"She says to go on over." He opened the door and pointed to the house.

"Can I bring my dog?" Pam looked at him with Boo snuggled in close to her.

"Oh course you can little lady."

We went out in the slushy mess that covered the gravel and made our way over to the inviting house. I could smell wood smoke in the air, which reminded me of our home. Ours had a grand fireplace that was the centerpiece of our living room and a gathering place that we loved.

A white-haired woman stood with the front door open and her hand on her skirt to keep it from blowing in the wind. A smile gently crossed her face, and she waved at the kids. "Come in, come in!"

I crossed the threshold and shut the door behind me. As I turned around, I could see the kids already in the living room with toys pulled out of box in middle of the room. They were not shy.

"I'm Anna." She tenderly touched my arm and took my coat. "Come in and have some hot tea. I already made some, expecting Howie any minute." Anna shuffled ahead of me and led me to her brightly lit kitchen.

"My name is Lou. It's so nice of you to open your home to us....We don't even know you."

My voice must have sounded concerned because she turned to look at me, and then took my hand in hers.

"The Bible is life's instruction book and teaches us to help those in need. Howie and I have welcomed many strangers over the years, and we've never regretted it! Do you like Earl Grey?" She held out a chair for me to sit and went for her teapot on the counter. "Kids do you want a cookie?" She raised her voice enough for the kids to pop into the kitchen.

"Thank you." Rusty took two cookies from the plate and handed one to Pam. They sat at the table next to me.

"I like Earl Grey." I held out my teacup and watched the steam rise from the china pot she held in her hands, which quivered lightly. "You mentioned the Bible. Are you a..."

I couldn't finish what I was going to say.

"Yes, I am. Are you?" Anna appeared frail, but her bold spirit shone mightily.

"I am. My husband and I are new Christians. We're moving to Alaska where he's going to Bible school." I tried to sound matter of fact and to not show any emotion.

"Hmm. Go ahead kids and play in the living room. I'll make you some hot cocoa and let you know when it's ready." Anna leaned forward and placed her hand over mine. "You don't want to go, do you?"

I hadn't wanted to be transparent, how did she know? I looked at my tea, then back at her. A tear formed in my eye. "I don't."

"Lou, I know because the same thing happened to me. Howie and I have been in love since we were kids." She waved her hand. "Anyway, we moved from another province for him to go to Bible school here in Alberta. It was long ago when you couldn't go home so easy." She repositioned herself in her chair. "I was so homesick, I cried for days on end. Finally, I had to lay it at Jesus' feet and trust that he would carry me." She pointed to herself and rested her hand on her chest. "Trust him, Lou. He'll carry you through. He'll always be near as you follow him. Take it from this old lady: the sooner the better!"

What were the chances we'd land at Anna and Howie's? I shook my head in disbelief at the haphazard way our paths had crossed. "Thank you."

"I'd say it's a divine appointment. Wouldn't you?" She smiled at me, raised her teacup, and took a sip. "Help to mend your vehicle and maybe a little tiny bit of balm for your soul to help carry you to Alaska, eh?"

Behind me, a door opened and I heard feet stomp. I turned to see Roy come forward a couple of steps and into the kitchen. He removed his hat, stepped to me, and put his hand on my shoulder. "I'm sure by now you've figured out that God sent us an angel!"

"Yes, indeed!" I smiled over at Anna who shrugged.

Howie went into the kitchen and opened one of the cupboards. "Would you like some tea, or should I put on some coffee?"

"I'd love a cup of coffee." Roy set his hat on his knee and looked around. "Thanks again for all the help! You have perfect timing."

Howie put the stovetop percolator on the burner and turned it on. "It's how it is with the LORD. His timing is best. So when you crossed the border, did you have any issues?"

When Howie asked the question, Rusty rushed in from the living room. "They only wanted to see Grandpa's gun."

"Oh really?" Howie put his arm on Rusty's shoulder. "How did it go?"

"Nothin' happened. They said it's neat, then asked Dad about it and about what other guns he had. I'm sure glad because Dad told me it'll be my gun one day, and I'd hate to leave it behind."

"Well, good. It looks like in a few hours you can all be on your way. We'll let the camper dry out a bit. Who wants to play a game?"

Boo barked from the other room, and we all laughed.

I looked around at all smiling the faces. What a joy to have family along the way!

THE FAN FROM THE HEATER RATTLED AND KNOCKED. Roy rolled over next to me and plopped his arm on my stomach. I let out an *Umph* and moved his arm.

"Roy." I waited to see if he was still awake.

Silence answered.

I replayed the events of the day with thoughts of the new friends we'd made. I also anticipated a visit with Fred and Julie when we arrived in Tok. The kids would enjoy the time. I had questions that I'd jotted down on my notepad to ask Julie. With our arrival at the end of October, I wanted to know more about winter and what she recommended. I didn't know how often we would go back and forth from Glennallen to Tok. I repositioned myself and hoped I might wake Roy up.

"Roy."

He let out a sigh. "Yes."

"I almost don't believe what happened today. What are the chances? The propane blows up, God sends us fellow Christians, and then they can relate to our move north." I rubbed my eyes and blinked.

"Yah." He rolled over and faced me. "It's true. We'll experience these impossibilities for the rest of our lives." He moved his arm and traced my hairline. "Feel any better?"

"I really needed to hear what Anna shared. I'm better. I'll try for you, for me, and the kids. I'm sorry for how I've been. It was so hard to leave."

"I know. It's one step at a time. Take one day at a time."

I closed my eyes and let the mantra wash over me. "One day at a time."

Help me, LORD, to offer You all my ONE days.

"Good night, Lou, get some rest." He held my cheek in his palm and fell asleep in a heartbeat.

Chapter 17

Welcome

I never would have believed I would make two trips to Alaska, and move to live in the north! I tucked my legs underneath me. My body ached from all the hours of travel, but the end was in sight as we prepared to cross over the border from Canada.

"What do you think our school will be like, Mommy? Will there even be any kids there? Will we walk, or ride the bus?"

I rolled my eyes and hoped Pam didn't notice. More and more questions barreled at me, most of which I didn't have answers for.

"Look! It's a cross!" Pam's finger jabbed my shoulder.

Perhaps it was an eighteen-wheeler whose lights shone right through the wispy clouds barely above the Welcome to Alaska sign. Whatever the cause, a perfect cross glowed in the clouds.

Rusty cleared his throat. "Wow, welcome to heaven!"

"How much better can it get? Bible school, learning about the Lord, a new home in Alaska. It sounds heavenly." Roy stopped the truck, and we all stared at the cross symbol in the reflection.

God, You are here with us.

"It reminds me of the rainbow God made for Noah after the flood," said Rusty. "My Sunday school teacher taught me that it means God will keep His promise to never flood the earth again. Is this cross a promise to us?"

Rusty's question was good one. What was it? A sign of God's presence with us? His provision? Or was there more we needed to cling to?

"Daddy, how much longer to Tok?" Pam's voice took on a whine.

I was eager to arrive there as well. Fred and Judy had invited us weeks ago to spend the night with them before we continued our travels south to Glennallen.

"Ninety miles, peanut. Not long at all. Maybe we should pull out a tape again to pass the time."

I opened my bag and picked out a tape. Our times of singing along to hymns had become a favorite for us. I'd try to find some keywords for the kids to find in the song, then we'd all try to find a verse to go along with it. As long as it kept them entertained. That was all that mattered.

It occurred to me that we would pass Miner's along the way. I swallowed a sip of tea for my dry throat. What would it look like in the winter? Would Birgit be working alongside her uncle? Would it even be open? I sang along as best I could for the next hour and noted how the windshield was slowly icing up. Perhaps it was even colder outside than when we stopped at Beaver Creek, close to the border in Canada.

As we approached Miner's on the left, Rusty noticed first. "Dad, there isn't any smoke from the stack. Do you think Brigit is there?"

He slowed the truck. "The driveway isn't plowed, so we

should go on. Hard to say what's happening. Maybe we can ask Fred what he knows."

It was solemn moment when we passed Miner's sitting frozen, lifeless, loafed in snow drifts and icy windows as though it was captured in time and waited to be born yet again. We continued to drive in silence. My memories turned to happier days at the roadhouse. Perhaps we all remembered pleasant days gone by. I was positive the time spent there would forever be a part of who we were as a family.

The familiar terrain of the next thirty miles brought back memories of our summer trip and the time we enjoyed in the Tanana Valley. Yet the season of winter brought on a whole new sentiment. A white world, with the snow heavy on the trees and blanketing the ground, making the earth look like it was resting in a deep slumber. It was truly winter here by the end of October.

"Mommy, will there be winter in heaven?"

I sure hoped not! I'd be quick to wish winter wasn't part of our forever existence. "I don't know," I said. "I hope for summer."

Thankfully, in our marriage Roy did most of the driving. I wasn't so sure about the winter driving conditions I would face. I knew the winters in Alaska would bring new challenges, so I changed the subject.

"We're not far from Tok now. Pick up your things. Have your boots and coats on," I said.

The ice on the windshield climbed up with accelerating speed and took over visibility. Roy took a fist to the dash and gave it a thud.

"What'd that do?" I questioned.

"Nothing, except make me feel better." He laughed at his own joke and pulled over to the side of the road. "I have to stop."

Now that we were nearly into the Tok community, the fuzzy

glow of some lights shone through the ice on the windows. Roy opened his door and stepped out. The rush of frigid air shocked me. How cold was it?

"Mommy, we're almost there!"

"Yes, but Daddy needs to see."

I leaned closer to the windshield and tried to pick out any movement outside. The entire vehicle felt frozen like an igloo.

He came back in, rubbed his shoulders and his knees, then clapped his hands in a movement he used in the cold to help get his circulation flowing. "It's freezing, and we'll look crazy, but we need to roll down the windows to look out the rest of the way. We're only about a half-mile from the church road. Ready, Lou?"

"OK?"

What else could I say? I turned the crank, and my window came down slowly, like the movement of a glacier receding against a rocky bed. I reached my head out as best I could. The sting of the cold pierced my ears and cheeks. I blinked to keep my eyes open. I knew Roy needed my help, and I took quick breaths, as best I could, of the frozen air, inhaling through my nose.

"C-c-clear on this side." My voice quivered as the icy air stung my throat.

The crunch of the tires on the snow-packed roads resonated into the vehicle.

We crept slowly down the rest of the roadway. Thank goodness it was still daylight as we trudged along the last leg of our journey. What an adventurous trip!

We turned at the corner. I saw the white church, a haven of warmth and refuge for our aching bodies, which rapidly froze from the cold air rushing into the truck.

Roy lay on the horn with a fist and pulled in front of the parsonage. The front door swung open, and our dear friend waved wide eyed at the sight of us with our heads out the windows!

Fred yelled out with his hands over his mouth like a megaphone, "Welcome to Alaska!"

"Thank you, Jesus!" Pam bellowed out, then sprung out the door and raced into the house.

I let out a deep sigh of relief and wound my window up even slower than when I'd rolled it down.

Yes, thank you, God, for a safe trip!

Fred held the door open and stretched out for my hand. "Go on in. I'll help him unpack. Stand by the stove and warm up."

As I climbed the stairs to the door, Judy came across the threshold. I covered my mouth with my hand and fought back the tears in my eyes. "Judy!"

We held each other in the doorway. Boo scrambled past, running and sniffing his way around, maybe to find Pam. At last, we'd arrived!

"Oh, hey there, little pup." Judy watched Boo make himself at home. "Come in."

She held my elbow and took me a few steps over to the woodstove. The heat was glorious, and I wanted to melt right into the tile floor beneath my feet. Judy rubbed my shoulders. "How'd you get so cold?"

"Our vehicle iced up, and we couldn't see." I smiled at how ridiculous we must have looked. "Roy and I hung our heads out the last half-mile so we could see." My body shivered, and I rubbed my hands together.

"Good land! It's close to thirty below out there. No wonder you're an ice cube!" Judy handed me an afghan off the back of the couch and draped it around me. "I'll get you something hot to drink. First, wrap yourself in this."

"S-s-sorry." I shivered from head to toe. Did all the sitting slow my circulation? To stimulate it, I bent my knees and kicked my feet.

"It's no problem." Judy waved a hand at me as she walked over to the kitchen.

Rusty walked in, holding the rifle that Roy's dad had given him when we left. His precious shooting iron. He was determined to be a mighty Alaskan hunter. I smiled at him as he passed me.

"I need to find somewhere safe to put this, Mom. I don't want it to freeze up." He searched the room with his eyes.

Judy held a mug out for me. "Rusty, we have a gun rack in our room. Here, I'll show you where it can go for tonight."

I wrapped my hands around the mug and let the steam warm my face. I thawed as the fiery liquid warmed my throat.

The thump on the outside stairs announced the men had retrieved our items. I opened the door for them.

Fred looked at the blanket. "Lou, you'll have to calibrate for the cold. I highly recommend that when you travel at thirty below, you wear your coat and boots, have your gloves handy, and—Never mind, we'll go over it all later." He set his hand on my shoulder. "It's good to have you here!"

Roy scanned the room. "Rusty, come back and help bring in the rest." He set our bags on the floor and watched me scoot away from the door. "Where are you running to?"

"The door lets in the frozen Alaskan air!"

He smiled and shook his head. "Rusty!"

"Coming, Dad! What else do we need to get?"

"Almost everything needs to come in. It'll freeze if it's left it out." Roy pointed his hand behind him at the truck and camper.

"Oh yah."

"Did you get your pea shooter out of the truck already?"

"Dad, it's a real rifle." He looked at the twinkle of mischief in Roy's eyes and then slipped his boots back on.

"Yah, buddy, it is." He gave Rusty a playful pinch on the shoulder.

Alaska promised the perfect backcountry for their keen,

passionate gun interests. I was glad for them, but what would I do in my unoccupied time?

"When you're all done, I have food ready." Judy wiped her hands on her apron and put her arm around my shoulder. "I'm so glad you came!" She pulled me in tight.

"Me too."

I meant it. I was glad to be at Judy and Fred's tonight! Although, I wasn't so sure about the next or the day after.

Chapter 18

HEAVENLY HOME

THE NEXT MORNING, I OPENED MY EYES AND
searched around the room. The log walls and small window
drew me back to where I was, in Tok, Alaska. The soft covers
invited me to linger in bed longer. However, I slipped out from
under their warmth and tiptoed over to my bag. Determined to
keep our trip crisp in my mind, I removed my notebook and
jotted down the date and time. If I thought of it, I'd make notes
of our drive today or special events to remember as we arrived
in Glennallen. I left a spot for the temperature reading on the
outdoor thermometer. Yesterday Judy had pointed to it, nailed
on a tree.

"Make sure you remember." I mumbled to myself.

"What?" Roy peeked over the covers at me.

"Just talking to myself. I don't want to forget to check the
temperature when we leave. It was so cold yesterday!" I shuddered at the memory of my core blasted with arctic air and the
interior of the truck encased in ice.

"Fred and I worked on the defrost. I hope it works now." Roy sat and scratched his head. "Lord willing, we won't see any other problems on our short drive. Then we're home free." He stretched his arms out wide and yawned. "Possibly three hours and we'll pass through the gates to our heaven on earth."

I drew back the curtains, and the sky revealed an ambient glow from the rising sun. The clouds sat high on the horizon, and the frosted trees glistened in the low light. As I pulled on a thick sweater, I remembered how swiftly I'd turned into an ice cube the day before. Judy told me the cold was more enjoyable when you were prepared for it. Back in Michigan, we experienced winters, but they weren't nearly as harsh. I knew we'd have a lot to learn.

Fred and Judy sat at the table and looked over an open book. They gazed at us with wide smiles when we stepped into view.

"Good morning! Hope you're braced for your next adventure." Fred's enthusiasm was amazing, and I could see how he was a good fit for Alaska, determined to take on most anything.

In the summer, when he had suggested we help at Miner's, it had sent me into a downward spiral. Now, we were headed for Glennallen with hopes of embracing a divinely appointed beginning.

"Bring it on." Roy pulled out a chair. His confident answer didn't speak for both of us.

There's peace in my heart, thank YOU, LORD. Please help me choose peace throughout the day.

I'd left Michigan a wreck, kicking and screaming on the inside. Safely in Tok, was I ready to press onward? I surveyed the room and smiled at how satisfied I was here with friends.

Judy stood and placed a plate of muffins on the counter. "Have one or two. We can wait for the kids to finish their game, and then we'll eat together." Judy pulled her oven mitts on. "Where will you live in Glennallen?"

"Thankfully, there is housing close, which means the kids can walk to school." I relaxed into a chair at the table.

Fred grasped my forearm and gave it a squeeze. "When you get there, you need to go to Faith Hospital. Tell the office manager to hire you!"

He must have noticed the incredulous look that flashed across my face. Why hadn't I sensed that Roy or myself may have to work a job? I figured the sale of the house might carry us for a while. Perhaps we'd overlooked our finances?

"Thanks, I'll keep it in mind." I peered over to see Roy's amused face, gazing at me. "What?"

"You should see what I'm seeing! You said, 'thanks' but your face said, 'no way!'"

Heat surged to my cheeks, and I shook my head. Easily embarrassed, I sipped my coffee and hoped there'd be a change of subject away from myself.

Judy touched my back as she passed me on her way toward the bedrooms. "Time for breakfast, everyone!"

A stampede of feet rushed in, with Boo trailing close behind.

Fred rose to his feet, and we all joined hands in prayer. "Heavenly Father, we thank You for the blessing of friends and family. Please continue to lead and guide the Wendels. Bless their obedience to You. Help them settle into Glennallen. Please give them good friends there. Thank you for the food that my beautiful wife made, and I pray in Jesus' name, amen."

A hum of amens filled the room.

They echoed in my heart.

Four degrees Fahrenheit at ten in the morning. I scribbled in my notebook as best I could on the bumpy road south out of Tok. The sun crested over the mountaintops ahead of us and invited us to continue onward.

"Mommy, how far to Glennallen?"

"Look for a road sign, Pam. I don't know."

"OK....Is it a long trip, Mommy?"

I glared into the back seat at her. "Look–out–your–window." The amount of patience left in me after traveling over ten days was scant. "Count how many cars you see." I gritted my teeth and hunted for some sign of how much longer until we weren't in the truck together anymore.

A raven flew across the treetops. There were so few birds compared to the summertime.

We jostled over a heap in the road, and I looked to Roy. "What was that?"

He held the wheel with two hands. "A frost heave. Fred warned me of a big one just outside of town. I guess they're common here. If you aren't alert, they might just toss your vehicle around. Can you find a tape for us to listen to?"

The truck rumbled across a bridge. Open water flowed in the middle of the river, while ice formed at the sides. We slowed at a pullout past the bridge.

"Daddy, what's that?" Pam's piercing question rang in my ears, and she pointed ahead of us to the mountains.

"They're called sun dogs," I said.

A rainbow wrapped the sun and sprayed color against the backdrop of the mountains.

"So that means there's gold in them there hills?" Rusty's twang resonated a certainty to hope for the best just over the horizon.

"Nah, uh, it means there's water!" Pam took offense, and the banter began in the back seat.

I thumbed the tape in as fast I could and turned up the volume. A parenting skill I used often.

"Look, Mommy, there're small tracks on the lake! What kind of animal was that?"

I pretended I was lost in the music. The stereo played "Turn Your Eyes Upon Jesus," and I listened with my eyes closed.

· · ·

O SOUL, ARE YOU WEARY AND TROUBLED?
   No light in the darkness you see?
   There's light for a look at the Savior,
   And life more abundant and free!

I KNEW THE CHORUS SO I HUMMED ALONG.

TURN YOUR EYES UPON JESUS,
   Look full in His wonderful face,
   And the things of earth will grow strangely dim,
   In the light of His glory and grace.

WHEN THE SECOND VERSE STARTED, I OPENED MY
eyes and peeked in the back seat. The kids had stopped their
exchange and looked out their windows. I placed my elbow on
my door and listened closely to the last verse.

HIS WORD SHALL NOT FAIL YOU—HE PROMISED;
   Believe Him, and all will be well:
   Then go to a world that is dying,
   His perfect salvation to tell!

*LORD, I'M SO GLAD YOUR WORD DOESN'T FAIL US. I HOPE TO LIVE IN
this world and show You to others. Help me keep my eyes on You.*

   I laid my head back on the seat and placed my elbow on the
door, where I cradled myself. If we went into full-time ministry
after Bible school, would Glennallen be one stop of many?
Where else would our family venture?

Somehow, I drowned out much of the trip and concentrated on songs as I tried to imagine more of what lay ahead of us.

We came to a long sweeping corner and two trucks parked on the side of the road.

"Mommy, it's truck number one!"

These were the first vehicles we'd seen on this lonely stretch of highway. Roy slowed the pickup to a crawl. Two men dressed in bulky gear with rifles slung over their backs looked ahead and toward the tree line. Out on the frozen lake, a caribou lay still.

"Dad, is it hunting season in the winter?"

"Rusty, there are winter hunts all across the state. Phew! Imagine hunting in yesterday's weather?"

The truck gained speed, and the kids chattered about hunting. Pam certain she'd never shoot the animals, and Rusty's views, of course, contrary to hers.

I pointed ahead. "Look, more caribou!"

On the road ahead of us, a herd of caribou scattered as our vehicle approached. The bulk of the herd hurriedly ran into the woods, and I saw a calf linger behind the others. It stopped to stare at us, then jumped and ran to join the group. We all laughed at the comical baby caribou who didn't seem to know what to do.

As we approached Glennallen, a small airport came into view. Fred had explained to us how aviation played a huge role in their ministry to places more difficult to access. He was familiar with many missionaries who used planes all over the state. The small planes frightened me. I watched one skip along the runway.

The next hymn that played was one we'd heard over and over the entire trip; however, this time , it pricked my ears. The second verse began:

WHILE WE WALK THE PILGRIM PATHWAY,

clouds will overspread the sky,
but when traveling days are over,
not a shadow, not a sigh.

TRAVELING DAYS OVER! AH YES, THAT'S A WELCOME THOUGHT!

WHEN WE ALL GET TO HEAVEN,
What a day of rejoicing that will be!
When we all see Jesus
We'll sing and shout the victory.

"MOMMY, IT'S A SONG ABOUT HEAVEN JUST AS WE GET to Glennallen!"

"I know!"

"Looks like any other town to me. When are we going to eat?"

"Rusty, I have the lunch Miss Judy made, and we'll eat when we get to the school." I concentrated on the road ahead of us, so grateful the trip was ending.

Earlier, Rusty had rubbed his gun down before storing it in the camper. As Judy watched him, she'd reassured me she thought we were prepared for our new Alaskan life. Rusty corrected her and said we were calibrated for Alaska. Her laugh was kind, and she noted she'd never thought of calibration in a way besides rifles.

What did it mean for the women of the north here in Alaska? Could we be calibrated for life here, or was that just the men?

I took out my notebook and placed it on my lap. With a sweaty hand, I held the pen and noted our trip with some bullet points. It was difficult to write while traveling those bumpy roads with frost heaves that tossed you around.

Arrived in Glennallen, Alaska. Roy, Pam, Rusty, Boo, and myself
Nov. 1, 1976.

Three plus hours driving from Tok.

Temp: 5F

I looked over at Roy. "I never thought we'd make it!"

"Home at last!" Roy cheered us on as we finished our last couple of miles to the school.

Home at last. It didn't feel like it. Home was Michigan where everything was familiar.

Chapter 19

NEW START

THE KIDS BANGED THEIR BOOTS ON THE PORCH. I SET my crochet work on the couch. Our new normal was setting in, in the two weeks since we'd finished our move.

"Mommy, I'm home!" Pam's arrival was never a surprise; however, she didn't want it missed. Her mitts flew through the air and landed on the washer nearby.

"Pam!"

"I'll put them away later. They're wet!" She yanked off her hat and gave it a mighty shake, flinging snow around.

"How'd you get so wet on such a short walk?" I brushed the snowflakes from her nose.

"They're wet from before. At recess they froze. Now they are just wet." Notorious for losing one of the pair, she added to her chatter. "I have both of them. Aren't you happy?"

I helped her with her coat, and she retrieved her mitts.

I walked to the small living room and set Pam's wet mitts on the tile in front of the woodstove. "If we put them by the fire, they'll dry out quickly. Rusty? How was your day?" I searched to see him.

"Uh, fine. I c-can't get these off!" The struggle in his voice grew, and I went to the entryway where he sat on the floor and pulled at his boot. "It's stuck!"

I held the boot between my legs while he yanked to pull his foot out. I tumbled backward onto the floor with the boot.

"Wow! Sorry, Mom."

"It's OK." I smiled at him and put my hand inside to feel the inner boot felts. "Rusty, your dad told you these must come out each night, or you'll freeze your feet. They get moist during the day, then freeze when you're outside. Try to remember. Now go set them by Pam's mitts."

There were many things to keep track of to defend against the Arctic temperatures, which battled us from every angle. Roy's mind was keen on ways to sidestep trouble, and he worked to help the kids and me be mindful as well. One minor mistake could have the most dreadful impact.

"I have some boiling water for cider," I said.

I took the mugs to the table. A neighbor had given us a welcome basket with a few homemade items, including a jar of cider mix, which I added to the hot water. It was a treat we all enjoyed. Sitting around the kitchen table, we sipped our hot drinks.

"How was school today?" I asked.

Our after-school routine had become one I looked forward to since it was something familiar amidst all the changes. The kids had made friends and adjusted to their new school.

Pam slapped herself on the forehead. "Today, there was a girl at school who called me a boy! She was home sick last week. The teacher told her, when she came today, that there was a new student and to say hi." She rolled her eyes and placed her elbow on the table.

Was the story too much to bear?

"She screamed, 'oh, there's a new boy!'" Pam stood and placed her hands on her hips. "I said, 'I am not a boy! I'm a girl with short hair!' And she was like 'ohh!'"

Rusty shook his head and laughed.

I raised my eyebrows at him, a quiet gesture that meant "no more."

"What's her name?" I picked up my cup and took a sip of the hot cider. The aroma of the cinnamon sweetly teased my nose.

"Betsie. She's OK." She stirred her cider and licked the spoon. "At recess she said sorry and we played. She told me I could call her Bestie if I wanted 'cause she'd be my bestie new friend!" She tilted the cup back, perhaps tasting the last drop, and set the mug down hard on the table. "We'll see about that!"

"Be easy on her. Maybe she'll be your best friend ever!" I hoped so. A best friend was a genuine gift.

"Rusty?" I asked.

"School is school."

More stomps sounded on the stairs, and the kids abandoned the table.

"Daddy!" Pam ran and slid on the linoleum into the entryway.

"Hey there, peanut. Hi, Rusty."

Roy walked over, carrying Pam. He gave me a kiss hello.

"Want some coffee?"

"Sure." He went to the living room, sat down, and put his feet up on a box we used as an ottoman. "I met a young man from Eagle today. You think Glennallen is remote! Remember the Taylor Highway that goes north of Tok? They don't maintain it in the winter. They fly in and out if they need to leave. He has stories! We should have him over for supper sometime. He can tell the kids what it's like growing up running a trapline, mushing a dog team, and ice fishing."

Rusty lay on the floor. "Wow, sounds fun! Dad? Can we do some trapping? I hear boys talk about it at school."

"Hard to say. Most trappers have an established line they trap. We're still new. We'd have to ask around to see if maybe someone has one they aren't using this winter. Starting our own would be expensive. We'd have to buy all the traps."

"A boy at school said the teacher trapped a lynx last year and brought it to school."

I picked up my crochet hook next to Roy. Crocheting was something easy to work on with little bits of time; I could pause a project and return to it when I had a moment.

"Pam met a friend today." I smiled at her while Boo gave chase around the living room with her.

"Yah, she guessed I was a boy!" Pam chased Boo down the hall and crashed into the boxes at the end. "Sorry, Mom!"

I shook my head and kept on crocheting.

"Speaking of boys…some guys at school are going on a short mission trip after Christmas. I think I'll go. It's not required for my class, but it will help us decide if I want to do full-time missionary work or not."

"Sounds interesting. Where to?"

"We'll fly to a small village to help with a winter project and lead some Bible studies. Fred will lead the crew. He's calling it a vision trip, to help students decide how to use their Bible knowledge, whether in daily life or in full-time ministry."

"It's great that Fred is leading it."

Roy moved closer to me on the couch and quieted his voice. "Do you think you can look for a job?" He raised his hand. "We're fine, don't worry. However, if we want to buy a piece of land, we should add to our nest egg."

I placed my crocheting work down and put my ring finger in my mouth to find a nail to chew. "I wouldn't know where to begin. Can you find something?"

"Lou, you're talented and determined. See what you find, and if nothing turns up, I'll consider driving a school bus or something. I've a lot invested in these classes."

I glanced around to see where the kids were, then checked my watch. Time to start supper.

"I'll see what I can do." I sauntered to the kitchen, washed and scrubbed my hands.

Was there another choice, other than me looking for work? Would it be too much to expect Roy to do school and work? I inhaled deeply and concentrated on cooking.

I ROSE EARLY TO PACK LUNCHES AND PREPARE breakfast. Then I paused in the kitchen. My notebook was close by, and I recorded the time and temperature. I peered out the window to check the thermometer gauge mounted to the window frame outside.

Huh? The radio announced minus ten, but our thermometer showed minus fifteen. It must have been muddled, because it didn't always line up with the forecast.

Roy came up behind me and rubbed my neck. "So, what do you think? Are you used to things here yet?"

I closed my eyes. The massage relaxed my tense muscles.

"I don't want to ruin everyone's excitement or crush our hopes, but it's different from what I imagined."

"I'd say it sizes up like most any other town. It's nice to study full-time instead of once a week at church and during Jim's visits." He turned me around to face him and held my hands in his. "I'll pray for your job hunt today."

"Thanks." I gave his hand a squeeze. "Yesterday, I heard about a job at the electric company. It's a short walk down the road from here, so I'll go to the office for an application."

"Daddy!" Pam ran down the hall and crashed into Roy's legs.

"What am I? Chopped liver?" I gave her a poke in the tummy.

"Mommy!" She pulled away from my tease, opened a

cupboard, and dragged out a loaf of bread. "Can I make my lunch?"

"Sure. What are you cookin' up?" I opened the fridge to pull out some ham for Roy's lunch.

"I'm makin' me a jam sandwich, and maybe I'll do one for Betsie!"

Rusty drew up a stool to the u-shaped counter. "That sounds gross."

"Nuh-uh! You just don't know how to cook!" She pointed a finger in his face.

"Finish your cooking, then come to the table, kiddos. Let's visit before we head out for the day." Roy sipped his hot coffee and gave me a thumbs up.

MY STOP AT THE ELECTRIC COMPANY WAS BRIEF SINCE the manager was out of town. I left the forms and my contact information. I zipped my coat to cover my neck and pulled my scarf over my mouth. I hoped I'd be warm enough while I walked the couple of blocks to Faith Hospital. At least I'd be able to tell Fred I'd wandered in.

I searched the road ahead. How bad could it be to take a brisk walk? The wind stung my thighs as I ventured along the snow-packed road. Perhaps this wasn't a good idea. I quickened my pace and tried to draw in shallow breaths to fend off the sting of frigid air in my lungs. My eyelashes frosted, and I blinked to see clearly.

A vehicle slowed behind me. I decided not to look back and continued my pace with one short block left. The car pulled up next to me, and the passenger rolled down their window. A woman with dark hair and bright blue eyes grinned at me.

"Do you want a ride? It's chilly today!"

"No, but thanks for stopping." I drew my scarf up higher on

my nose and wondered why I hadn't answered yes. It was only ten below, and I'd learned that the cold in the Arctic could plummet to fifty below or colder. How would I survive?

The hospital came into view, and I searched for the front door. I put my gloved hand over my face to help warm the air and jogged to the entrance.

I opened the door to the divinely warm waiting area of the hospital. My hood fell down, and my hair filled with static, the dry air making my hair stand on end. How lovely was that? Did I even care anymore after the coldest walk of my life?

I set my gloves on a seat and tugged off my huge coat. I blinked and tried to stop the water that was running down my face. I touched my cheek with my palm and saw black goo on my fingers. The frost from my eyelashes took my mascara right along with it. I must be a sight!

"Hello."

"Hi." I turned as I answered, even though I'd hoped to locate another exit out of there fast. A slim woman stood in the waiting room.

"Can I help you?" She clasped her hands in front of her and smiled at me.

"I'm so sorry. I must look awful." I brushed at my hair and tried to mat it down, but it rose on end with each attempt to flatten it.

"We don't fret about that here. Winter has a way of messing with everything. Do you have an appointment?"

"No." I glanced around the narrow room with chairs and scripture verses matted in frames of pictures with landscape photography. I'd not seen a hospital like this before. "I'm Lou. My husband and I moved here last week. He's going to Bible school. I was out for a walk and stopped to warm up." I hoped it was OK to enter without a decent reason.

"Out for a walk? It's nearly twenty-five below out there! Please stay as long as you need. My name is Dana." She took my hands in hers and hesitated to hold them. "Sheesh, you're cold! Would you like some coffee?"

"Twenty-five below? Wow! My thermometer at home said ten." I rubbed my shoulders with my hands to warm them from the chill. "It sure seems colder."

"You'll discover the temperature varies here in town. If you live up on the hill, it may be much warmer there then down here. The cold air sinks and settles into the lower spaces. Follow me." Dana motioned for me. "Leave your things here. They're fine." She led me down a short hall and past a nurses' station and some patient rooms.

What a quaint hospital. The familiar scent of chicken soup made me feel more like I was visiting a home, not a clinic.

Dana went over to the coffeemaker, poured two cups, and handed one to me.

"I'm so glad you came in. I enjoy meeting new families who move here. Whether it's with the mission, the radio station, or the Bible college, there are fresh faces each year."

In the distance, I heard a telephone ring and Dana jumped, almost spilling her coffee.

"Oh, it scares me each time!" She wiped her lip with her hand. "It's the nine-one-one phone. The calls come through here, and the nurse listens in to determine if she needs to dispatch the volunteer ambulance crew or not. As you can see, this is a unique place!"

"Everything about Alaska has been unique so far. I think I'll be getting used to it for a long time."

As I finished my sentence, a tall man walked into the kitchen. "Hi, Dana." He glanced at me, then back at Dana. "Smells good in here. Suzie made her homemade chicken soup again."

"This is Lou. Her family is new in town."

"Lou?" He looked at me and grinned real wide. "I was warned about you." He nodded his head and held out his hand.

I shook his hand, then remembered my crazy hair and mascara-strewn face. What kind of impression was I making?

"Fred told me you'd stop in and ask for a job."

"Oh." Cornered in the kitchen, I faced friendly, but new people, and I searched for what to do.

"I'm Bill, the office manager here at Faith Hospital. I'd like you to—if you don't mind"—he smiled at Dana—"come with Dana and me to my office, and I'll talk to you about a secretary position I have open."

"I was out for a walk, and thought I'd stop in...I wasn't looking..."

Obviously, Fred knew Bill. Also, Bill knew Fred, which meant I was stuck! Bill waved at me. "No need to apologize. Not for a second. I've meant to hire someone who can help get things organized, and you come highly recommended by a respectable friend."

Did everyone know all about everybody here? This was an even smaller town than I'd lived in, and I felt like people knew us even before we arrived. I wouldn't have been polite if I didn't at least hear what he had to say, so I swallowed a mouthful of coffee and looked up at Bill, who questioned me with his eyes.

"Yes, I'll do the interview. You're sure now is an OK time?"

I hoped he would say "come again later" and give me a chance to think and prepare myself for any probing I may or may not have an answer for.

"Now's fine. Dana, will you please come along, and bring some of those cookies Suzie made earlier. They smell too good to leave behind. Suzie is our cook, and she spoils us."

I followed Bill and Dana back toward the front door. Deep down, I wasn't sure if I should thank Fred or not. I figured I'd have days, maybe weeks of looking and waiting for work. This happened faster than I could process.

I sat next to Dana. This was informal, like most things in Alaska. Something we'd noticed already in our brief stay. People wore the clothes that were most comfortable for them, and obviously, that wasn't any different in Faith Hospital. They weren't taken aback by my appearance or haphazard stop. The causal family atmosphere drew me in, and I prayed silently for God's guidance.

Help me, LORD. Is this from You?

"There isn't much to the interview, except some simple questions. I'll leave this paperwork for you to go over with Dana, and tomorrow you can come at, say, nine?" He slid some papers across his desk and crossed his arms. "From what Fred told me, you'll be an excellent fit here. Lord willing, a permanent part of Faith Hospital for years to come."

Years? I was looking for short-term work. "Thanks, I'll have a look at them. I need to talk to my husband first. Can I call you later?"

Bill raised himself out of his chair and stood in the doorway.

"Tell me tomorrow, when you come at nine." He walked away, and Dana and I looked at each other.

I listened to the sound of his footsteps fade away.

"I think you have a job, Lou!"

"I only stepped in for a minute!" I blinked and looked around the room.

Dana laughed. "It's possibly one of the most important minutes so far in your brief time here. Finding a job in a small town can be a challenge, especially as winter approaches. Pray about it, but I think this is a divine appointment." Dana put her hand on my shoulder. "Now, let's go over the forms and see how I can help you."

After scanning the documents and conversing with Dana, I went back for my coat. Dana handed me copies along with a napkin of fresh cookies to take home.

There would be a learning curve if I decided to take the job, but the warmth of the family atmosphere drew me to ask God *for* the job instead of *whether* I should take it.

Chapter 20

LAND

"MOMMY!" PAM'S WHINE FOR ME FROM THE OTHER room sent a piercing pain up my neck and into the base of my head.

Her whining had become more normal, and I'd have to discuss how to encourage a change in her tone with Roy. I stayed in my seat on the couch and waited for Pam to find me instead of going to her—a method I hoped would help her see I didn't run to her beckoning.

"MOMMY!"

Sheesh, that girl! I repositioned myself and tucked my knees in under myself to save my warm feet from the cold floor.

She came out of her room and marched in front of me. "Mommy." Her glare told me she meant business.

"Yes, Pam." I whispered to her in hopes of her mirroring the response.

"My pants are frozen!"

"Frozen?"

"Yes, to the wall!" She plopped down on the floor, criss-crossed her legs and folded her arms.

"When your Dad gets home with Rusty, you can show him. I'm sure he'll know what to do." I rubbed the back of my neck.

Why did this evening drag on? Was it because it got dark so early in the afternoon?

"If this is heaven, why is it so freezing here!" She threw herself onto a large pillow on the floor and wiped her face with her hand.

I heard Roy's whistle, so he and Rusty had to be outside.

"Honey, it isn't heaven."

Pam let out a theater award-winning sigh. "And Betsie was no angel today, so I've been wonderin' about this whole heaven thing."

"Betsie was no angel? How about you, Pam? Were you a perfect angel in school? Did the teacher ask you to stop talking when she was? It's best not to point the finger at someone else. Now get up and find your pajamas for bed."

Traveling with sloth speed, she trudged down the hall. I supposed I hadn't satisfied what she'd hoped to gain from her performance.

The boys shut the door with such force the trailer shook.

"This door!"

Roy's frustrated voice reminded me of another item we needed to discuss. A stove top that didn't work when the temperature plummeted to thirty below. I scrounged for a pot I could use on the woodstove.

Boo shook off the cold and chased his tail. He must have come in with the guys when they'd arrived home from the Bible school meeting.

Rusty appeared from the hall. "Hey, Mom."

Roy sauntered over, whistled a tune, and sat next to me. He reached his icy hands to my neck, and I pulled away from him.

"Oh no you don't!"

"Give me one minute to warm..."

He inched closer, but I jumped off the couch and startled Boo. He barked at me and ran away.

"I'll get you a nice hot cup of coffee instead. How was the meeting?"

"Great. Can I tell you more later? At supper you said your job hunt went well. So?"

I pulled out a cookie from the jar and brought it with Roy's coffee. "Fred had already called the clinic, so when I stopped in to look around, I met the office manager. He knew all about me." I gave Roy the gingersnap and popped one in my mouth. "He offered me a job." I let the words linger and waited for him to ask more.

"Perfect timing, 'cause tonight at the meeting someone told me about some property we can buy. It's a great location, and there's already a cabin on the lake." He held out his palm. "Don't be stingy with the cookies. Are there more?"

I gave him a half-smile and raised my eyebrows. I had hoped the cookies would last longer than one evening. Oh, well. I went for a couple more and placed them on a napkin. The kids crept quietly into the kitchen. They grinned at me and begged with their eyes.

"Oh OK. Have a seat." I handed them two each and moved to the couch.

"The truck will need some parts since this cold weather has taken its toll. After the repairs, let's go for a drive to the property. Can you picture it? A log home nestled on a lake, caribou escorting their young across the frozen waters, and loons singing nearby in the summer." He placed his arm around my shoulder and pulled me in. "Doesn't it sound perfect?"

"On a lake?" Pam asked with her mouth full. She stuck her hand over her open mouth. "Sorry"

She got off her chair and joined Roy. "Daddy, if we live there, will my pants still freeze to the wall?"

"Where'd that come from?" He reached for Pam and placed her on his lap.

"You'll have to go to her room and see what you can do." I hoped he noticed the exhaustion in my voice because I was ready to call it a day. Perhaps the cold weather drew the life out of person. When we'd lived in Alaska for a while, would our bodies acclimatize and calibrate for it? "Where's the property?"

"A mere thirty-five miles out of town."

I sat up straight, looked into his eyes, and blinked. I pulled at my ring finger and gave my wedding band a spin. "You're joking?"

"Nope. Sounds perfect to me." He bounced Pam on his knee. She flew off and landed on the floor, giggling.

"Dad, we could trap on our own land!" Rusty came near us. "Can we hunt there too?"

The kids asked more questions. I tuned them out and gazed at the frost on the living-room window pane. This frigid world gripped me with force and left me breathless. My right hand in a fist, I pressed at my lips, resolved to find the strength to move forward from this frozen place.

"My Father, which gave them to me, is greater than all; and no man is able to pluck them out of my Father's hand." The Bible verse Faith shared with me came to mind.

Yes, I'm in the Father's hand!

Warm me, Father. Help me, Father.

Don't let go!

"OK, let's hold hands and pray before bed."

Roy's firm hand rubbed my back as I leaned forward to bow my head. He stroked me reassuringly as we prayed. The kids snuggled close into a group hug. He knew me well. I'm sure he saw my face. I was pleased that he kept the mood light and closed the day with prayer.

※

After breakfast the next morning, I saw the kids off to school, then bundled up, walked down to Faith Hospital, and signed paperwork to start my new job. As I walked out the door and returned home, I smiled at the opportunity to serve the Lord with my new employment. The hospital served as a medical mission, which was something I'd never heard of.

Well, LORD, You gave me the job, and You'll be the one who helps me do it, even if it's for a short time.

The next item on our to-do list was to have the truck fixed and to look over the property for sale. Roy came home early from school with truck parts in his hand that he'd bought from a friend. His excitement about a trip to the property had the kids racing around the snow piles out front while they waited for the truck to be ready.

We put our warm clothes on and buckled in. A lesson we'd learned when we drove up the highway was to be prepared in case the vehicle had any issues. Roy, the kids, and I sang along to the radio. We all enjoyed the Christian radio station that broadcasted from our new town. I tucked the blanket under my legs and bobbed my knees to help keep them warm in the truck.

The drive out to the property seemed to take forever; maybe because it was such a big decision. I fixed my gaze out the window and watched the trees pass mile after mile. My hands gripped together to stay warm. I'd discovered they hurt when they turned cold and stung as they warmed up. I wanted to conceal my apprehension about a move so far out of town.

The road stretched out, taking us farther away from civilization. After a sharp turn to the right, we entered the driveway amidst a forest of small spruce trees.

"Is that the house?"

Pam's question echoed within my head. Ahead, near the lake, stood a small cabin. Would it be home? Boo's bark from the back seat, announcing he was eager to get out and run around.

"C'mon Boo." Rusty opened his back door and let in the cold winter air.

I wrapped my scarf in closer to my neck and went out.

"Look! There are such cute Christmas trees here!" Pam ran over to the wooded area behind the cabin.

"Stay close, Pam." Roy walked over to the cabin, and I followed behind.

I shook my head, glad no one could see the doubt within me. Would we live this far from town and commute to school and work? When we lived at Miner's, I couldn't imagine how the kids would take the bus twenty miles to Tok if we'd stayed, and this was much farther.

Roy reached for the knob and opened the door to the cabin. I stepped in and heard the rumble of a vehicle in the driveway. Inside, I noted the small space while Roy turned to go out and meet the seller.

A temporary fix from where we lived now? I wrinkled my nose at the musty smell. Once we started a fire in the room, would it smell more appealing? I touched the rough countertop, which wasn't over eight feet long, with a stove on one end and fridge on the other. The muffled voices of the men greeting one another carried over in the cold air. I turned and inched toward the doorway to listen.

"It's five acres with access to the lake. We lived here short-term and now we have a home up the road. There's phone and power already, so that's a bonus. Normally, you pay more if you have to put those services in on your own. We'd be happy to see your family here."

How nice for him to want us to be happy. Would we be?

"Oh, there isn't running water! Not sure if I mentioned that when we talked."

I took a step outside as the shock of his words rattled my

weary legs. I held onto the door frame as I stepped out. How'd you live out here without water?

"Hi, I'm Adam."

Bundled in his parka and stocking hat, Adam stood close to the same height as Roy. He sounded friendly. I wondered how his family had managed with so little.

"Hi, I'm Lou." I waved since I didn't take off my mitts for a handshake. "Maybe because I'm new here, I don't understand... How do you manage without water in the winter?"

Adam scanned the lake, then returned his gaze to me. "Well, either you haul it or"—he pointed to the lake—"you melt it. I hear your family is adventurous. Even took a turn at running a roadhouse. Eh! You'll get it all figured out without a hitch!" He swung his arm toward the cabin. "It heats well with the stove. I just cleaned the stack last week. Hey, look around and show your kids. I'll wait if you have questions."

Where did this casual you've-got-this kind of attitude come from around here? Folks took on the grandest projects and lifestyles, then shrugged as though it was no big deal.

I raised my eyebrows in Roy's direction. "I'll go check on the kids." Their voices, in cheery tones, carried from behind the cabin. What had captured their attention?

The cabin didn't seem more than twelve to sixteen feet long. I used my stride to guesstimate as I followed the kids' tracks.

"Mommy, we found some treasures!"

The kids knelt over some antlers in the snow.

"I think there's moose here and some caribou. Do you think they will let us keep them?"

Of course Rusty would like these trophies!

"Not sure. What else have you found?"

I scanned the woods behind me where the outhouse tucked near the edge of the trees. Now there was a treasure. *Humph*, I couldn't imagine what that was like in winter.

"We've seen animal tracks, and Rusty says there are traps

over there by that shack!"

"Shack?"

"Yah, there're a couple of buildings over there. I don't know what for. It's so cool out here, Mom! Do you think we'll move here?"

"Mommy's face says no." Pam rubbed the antlers with mittens like she was shining them. "I think it'd be fun to live here and have all this snow for just us!"

"It's a decision we will pray about, Rusty." I felt a tear sting my eye.

Why did everyone else just jump into these fresh adventures, while I hung on the sidelines? I rubbed my hands on the log walls and pretended to examine them closely so the kids wouldn't spot my emotion. I shuddered at the thought of thawing frozen water for household use, and the immense work it'd take for simple tasks.

I folded my arms around my torso as best I could and hoped to warm myself from the slight breeze that blew off the lake.

Roy's whistle echoed from the front of the cabin. I slowed my pace and gazed at the trees, giving myself time to gain composure. There was beauty in this wilderness. Could I grow to enjoy it? Yes, on the other side of the windowpane next to a warm fire! This frozen land beckoned the outdoorsman. How did an indoorsy-type like myself fit in?

I tried to blink back tears as I came close to the front of the cabin.

"Thanks, Adam!"

Adam waved to me from his truck and headed for the highway.

"What do you think, Lou?" Roy's eyes were wide and his arms were flung out at his sides. He seemed excited.

"It's an interesting idea." I looked back at the cabin.

He took my hand. "I'm serious—it's a great deal!"

"There isn't any water. We would live like in the olden days!

I can't imagine my life here." I bit my bottom lip and tried to hold back the tears that forced their way down my cheeks.

He swung my hand, still clutched in his. "You'll do just fine. There are simple solutions to a temporary issue. We can haul water from town, melt snow, the kids can take showers at school. I can use one at the school and the hospital has one. It's not uncommon here. Plus, this is the perfect spot, right on our very own lake! You'll have all the water you could ever hope for in the summer!"

My chilled body shivered, and my mind demanded another option. "For the winter. In the spring, after school is over, can we find something else?"

"Like the roadhouse, your first reaction is to give a short-term commitment."

The kids came closer off the lake. They threw snow up in the air and danced under it as it fell. "Right. I need to try it first."

He let go of my hand and placed each of his on my shoulders. "It's a money-saving option, and a place to live without restrictions. I'm sure if the winter is horrible, selling this wilderness paradise won't be a problem."

"Mommy, watch me ice skate!" Pam skirted herself on the ice and flailed her arms to keep balance.

"Let's make it work this winter," said Roy. "But I think we should buy it and keep in mind that, if all else fails, we can sell it."

"See, Mommy!"

I wiped my eyes with my mitten, forced a smile, and waved at her. I looked up at the sky turning pink from the sun on the horizon. "OK, I'll try it."

I'd whined like Pam did earlier, my hesitant heart questioning myself and our Alaskan adventure. God had opened the opportunity for Roy to attend school, he'd provided me with an outstanding job, and He was caring for our needs. Wasn't it time to let HIM work in me without a fight?

Chapter 21

New Ways

THE ICE BROKE AND CLAMORED ACROSS THE LAKE, shattering as it strewn close to the edge.

Challenges greeted us each day as we forged our way in this wilderness. The kids threw the chunks in hopes that they would shatter into pieces small enough to manage. We melted them on the woodstove, but only those small enough to fit in the oversized pot. Boo chased the shards as they fell and barked at them to make sure they didn't attack the kids.

"Put them in the sled!" I called out and hoped they would hear me from where I stood outside the door. The wind blew from the north across my face, reminding me we neared our coldest days yet this winter.

I watched the kids drop the ice on the sled, and Pam hopped on for the ride. Rusty swung the rope crisscross around his chest and pulled. The chore seemed to delight them. I doubted their delight would last much longer.

The door shut with ease, and I stared around at the one-room cabin we now called home. Simple, warm and comfortable. It was the most hurried housing decision in our marriage, yet, somehow, the easiest, since the five acres, cabin, and whatever else lay resting under the snow was all ours. Being debt-free lifted a weight I carried in a way I hadn't thought possible.

I heard the kids dump the ice into the wooden crate Roy had built. Our morning routine on the weekends included hauling ice and helping move firewood from where it was chopped.

"I said, it's the best I can do!" Pam's voice carried through the thick log walls.

She was so easily irritated these days. I wondered if there was something else I should do to help her. Was she getting enough sleep? The stress of many changes hung over each of us. My shoulders felt heavy as I walked to the front window to see if I could spot Roy hauling wood across the lake. At the lake's edge, Rusty waved. I returned a smile as he pulled the sled over the ice in the direction Roy had ventured.

A rush of cool air filled the cabin as Pam pushed the door open in a slump. "I'm done!" She yanked her woolen mittens off and tossed them across the room, then fell to the floor to yank off her boots. "Mommy! Take them off!"

I moved to her and looked at a pile of snow caked on her hat. "I'm happy to help you when you're polite." I waited and counted in my head to keep my composure for the little girl bursting at the seams with life.

"Mommy, please take off my boots." She grunted and pulled on them.

I reached to help and eased them off her tiny feet. "What's your deal there, little lady? Are you tired?"

I grabbed a chunk of snow off her hat, opened the door and threw it as far as I could.

"I'm cold, and I'm tired."

I held her cool hands and rubbed them together. "Go stand over by the fire. I'll make you something hot to drink. After lunch, I think a nap is a good idea."

I felt her forehead. Was there a fever brewing? She was a little warm to the touch. I placed my cheek to her face. It was hard to tell since she was flushed from her efforts outside and the air was cool but not as cold as it had been recently. I'd check on her again later.

Our third weekend in our cabin took us well into December. This remote, quiet life was growing on me, but I still considered this home as temporary.

I looked over at the calendar. I needed to make a handful of Christmas cards to send out soon. "Pam, do you want to help me make some cards?"

"No." Her pouting bottom lip sent me an obvious message to leave her alone.

Boo barked at the door, and I hurried to let him in. The guys must not have wanted him underfoot while they hauled wood.

I hummed as I gathered a few things for my craft. Who would we get cards from for our first Christmas away? Would a string along the wall be a fun way to display them where the kids could see? The week before, some ladies from work had invited me to create some homemade gifts. It was so nice to linger and laugh over futile attempts to Hodge Podge some jars for decorative lights. I smiled at the memory, hoping there would be more time to spend with new friends—a bright spot in the dark of winter.

I mingled some paper and glue, then pretended not to notice Pam tiptoe up the ladder to the loft. I heard the rustle of her down blanket and soon after, stillness.

Thank YOU, LORD, she's asleep.

"Mom, we're gonna shoot Grandpa's rifle!" Rusty's ecstatic announcement ushered him into the house, and he stood wide eyed, scanning the room with the door wide open.

I rose up from the table and shut the door behind him. "Rusty, close it as soon as you come in. It cools off in here fast."

"Wanna come watch?"

"Pam's asleep. I'll watch from the window. Here, I'll get it for you." I stood on the chair and laid my hands on the gun strapped above the entry.

Roy assured me we'd want it close, ready to grab in a hurry. Its only purpose, so far, was for Rusty to pine over.

He spun on his boots and grabbed the door handle. "I've been waiting for this all my life!"

I smiled at the door, which slammed in my face. Could anything stand in the way of a young boy shooting a gun for the first time?

I moved my chair over in front of the large picture window. Thankfully, the cabin's windows didn't frost over as much as the ones where we'd lived before. A clear view of the boys at the edge of the lake was a quintessential image I hoped to impress on my memory of our first days here.

They handled the rifle, their breath rising in the air in tiny clouds of moisture. It looked like Roy would shoot first, with Rusty behind him.

The rifle shot startled me, and I blinked. "Whoa." I spoke aloud to myself.

Boo growled and yipped at the window. He knew a shot fired might mean a squirrel for him.

"Shh, Boo!" Roy's shot across the lake must have hit the target because Rusty jumped and threw his arms high in the air.

The stock of the rifle lowered, and the instruction. I'm sure serious words were exchanged as they went over the basics of gun safety.

I heard a bump on the floor above me where Pam slept. Perhaps the shot had awakened her?

I repositioned myself so I could put my feet up, and balanced a book on my lap for a firm place to write on a card.

More antics between the boys—it appeared Rusty steadied himself on a log to take his first shot. Was he holding his breath like me? I saw the moisture freeze in the air from his exhale, and then the recoil of his shot sent him back into Roy's guiding arms. He leaned forward, froze in place, then swirled around to give his dad a high five. He looked to me, where I now I stood clapping! Rusty handed the gun back over to Roy, then ran to the house with Olympic speed.

The door swung open, and Rusty stood panting. "Mom! Did you see?"

"That was great!" I went to him and reached out for a hug. His cold coat pressed against me, and I felt his arms shaking.

"Dad says you're next, come out."

"Funny." I went over to my chair and moved it to the table.

"I think he's serious. He told me to remind you to dress warm." Out the door he went, leaving the frozen air inside, cooling off the cabin.

The sudden chill sent an icy shiver down my back. Me? I didn't shoot, and hadn't planned on it. Why did I have to go?

What kind of rifle was it, anyway? Would I ever need it? I looked out the large window, and Roy must have been watching for me, because he waved abruptly. I shrugged, then shuffled to the base of the ladder to the loft. There wasn't any movement. I guessed Pam was fine by herself with us outside. I dug around for my coat that hung on one of the hooks and put on my mitts. I pulled the ruff of my hood up and let out a sigh.

"Stay, Boo." I patted him on the head before I left the warm cabin.

The snow crunched beneath my feet, and my eyes squinted in the sunshine. I could barely see the lake with the bright snow reflecting in the light.

Roy stood with his chest puffed out, the rifle cradled in his arms.

"Lou, the gun doesn't bite!" He patted the log next to him.

Rusty cheered me on. "C'mon, Mom. It will be great!"

"Why do I need to shoot?" I clenched my teeth and hoped my irritation wasn't too obvious. There were many new things to learn, like how to function without running water. What purpose did this serve?

Roy pulled on my tense elbow. "You'll need to be comfortable. If you ever have to protect our family or property, you can't fumble around. I guess you could say this is part of your Alaskan calibration."

Wasn't it all part of calibrating to Alaska? Only one set of neighbors in one direction, and the rest was the vast wilderness. I curled my toes in my boots and crossed my legs one over the other. These dumb boots weren't designed for the cold. They were fine for going back and forth into town in the truck or for shopping, but I needed something else if I was going to be outdoors for long.

I looked around and raised my voice. "There's nothing I'll need to shoot. We live out here in the middle of nowhere."

Roy waved Rusty back closer to the house.

"You can do it, Mom!"

"Lou, I'll talk you through it and shoot a few times. Then we'll come out another time, and you'll do it all over again."

"Huh!" I forced out a laugh. Not likely.

He wrapped his left arm over my left shoulder, slid my left arm down, and placed my hand on the front of the stock. The gun, heavy in my hands, made my elbow ache as I attempted to hold still. He drew my limp right hand near the trigger and tilted the gun toward him. "This is the safety. It's on. Red means hot and ready to fire. You can see that it's black now, so you can't pull the trigger."

"I know how to shoot a gun." I narrowed my eyes and moved my face close to his cheek, which brushed against mine.

"Get the gun up close to your cheek and look down the site. See the target I put over there?"

"Um-hmm." The cardboard box stood in the middle of the lake, repositioned after Rusty's shot, and I clearly saw the circle I needed to aim for.

"Breathing and shooting go hand in hand. Release the safety, then take in a deep breath and keep your sight on target. Let out your breath slowly, then inhale again. Pause, then shoot. I'll talk you through it."

I clicked the safety off, and it sparked my desire to end this forced shot. A slow breath in, and I thought of the mantra "calibrating Lou!" Then a reluctant breath out—a pause like he said, and the sound of the loud, powerful gun as it fired.

The force sent me back in his arms, which were ready for me. How would I ever manage this without him? I didn't even see him load the thing. I pushed my hair away from my eyes, where it fell after the shot.

"Good! Let's try again. Next time see if you can hit the target." Roy took the gun from my hands and kept the barrel pointed to the ground.

"What? I didn't hit it?" I peered as best I could at the box on the frozen lake. I was so sure my aim had been true!

Stupid gun.

My feeble attempt to look closer at where my shot had traveled halted with Pam's sobbing cries, which shattered the icy air. I spun on my slippery boots and my feet fumbled to move as fast as I could to where she stood on the porch. Her uncontrollable sobbing sent me into a panic. Boo had wrestled out of the partly-open door and whined next to her. Rusty and I ran to her on the well-worn path from the lake to the cabin. He held her as she tried to push past him without a coat. She reached her arms out and wailed.

"Pam, I'm here!"

Her eyes were closed and puffy. Her face blazed red. And sweat dripped from her temples.

"It's OK, Rusty. I've got her."

He stood with his mouth open. "She must have a fever."

I opened the door and tried to scoot her in. How long had she cried? I'd sensed earlier that she was unwell. Why had I left her?

I heard Roy call for Rusty to help carry a few things up to the cabin.

"Shh." I gently nudged Pam to the couch and eased her down. As I held her hands, I felt the heat from her body radiate up my arm.

Dear God, how could she be so hot so fast?

I hurried to get a cool cloth for her head, then heard the boys come in, whispering to one another. Did they hear the panic in Pam's cries?

Roy came in and knelt next to her without taking off his boots. "What's going on?"

"She's burning up!" I handed him the rag, and he placed it on her forehead and stroked it down her face.

Pam moaned.

"My little peanut. Shh, it's OK." Roy stroked her hair.

"I don't have a thermometer." Our minimal belongings were sufficient for our basic needs, but we still had household goods to replenish. "I'm calling Kim. She's down the road a few miles." I dashed for the phone on the wall. Kim was an RN from the hospital. Surely she had a thermometer at home for her large family of five kids.

Lord, let her be home. Let her be home.

After the third ring, she picked up. I burst into tears and tried to talk. "Um, this is Lou." Thank God it was Kim who answered. "Do you have a thermometer? It's Pam, she's so hot!

I've felt anyone with a fever this hot... please!" Did she hear the plea in my voice?

"I'll be right there, Lou. I'll pray as I drive. Get her into dry clothes and have her sip some water. She's God's child, Lou. He knows. OK?"

"OK."

The click of the phone on the other end pricked my ear. Help was on the way. No—help was already here. God is always with us.

LORD, help Pam now. Please help her fever go away! Amen.

I stood and stared at my little girl. Her pitiful face drew me to hold her. To keep her close and safe, always!

FINALLY, HOURS AFTER KIM GAVE HER SOME MEDICINE to bring down the fever, Pam spoke calmly and rested comfortably in Roy's arms. The kids snuggled on the couch with Boo curled up in Pam's lap.

"Oh, Daddy." She let out a deep sigh. "My head isn't sore now." She cradled it on his chest.

"Good girl," he said. His eyes fluttered. Maybe he was falling asleep?

I brought over a cup with some soup I had made earlier. "Here Pam, sip on this. It's one of your favorites. Oh, sorry, Rusty. I almost tripped over you." I sat at Roy's feet. Rusty sat close by, flipping through a hardcover book.

"Hey, Dad? Do you think we could set those traps up tomorrow after church?"

"Huh? I was almost asleep." Roy rubbed his eyes with one hand. "Probably not since I have a mission-trip meeting tomorrow after church. It'll be dark by the time it's over. Draw a map of some ideas where we can go. Then we'll have a plan."

"Ah, yah!" Rusty jumped up and went to the table. His

sudden movement scared Boo, and he leaped from the couch to follow him.

"What are the dates?" I picked up my crocheting and watched Roy try to accommodate himself on the couch with Pam, who hardly let him move an inch.

"Fred suggested after Christmas, but if the weather is good, it may be sooner. He doesn't want to go if the temperature drops."

"I'll need to let the hospital know so they can find a replacement for me. The kids will be out of school."

"Daddy?" Pam wiggled away from Roy while she drank her soup.

"Yes, peanut?"

"Are you gonna be a missionary?"

"Well, I don't know. Your mom and I are praying God will answer that question. That's why Mr. Fred called it a vision trip."

"You ARE a missionary, Daddy. Already."

I smiled at Roy. Where was Pam's five-year-old reasoning going?

"Really?" He eased off the couch and walked to the coffee percolator, which bubbled on the woodstove.

"You're a missionary to *me!*" Her voice raised high, and she sat up tall. "You take care of me, and you take care of Mommy and Rusty."

"I like that. I like that a lot." He gave Pam a wink and whistled a familiar Christmas hymn.

Chapter 22

CARDS

One last task and I'd be done at work for the day. I typed out the notes from the latest board meeting and filed them in their place. My eyes scanned the waiting room just outside my office. It wasn't that long ago that I'd wandered in frozen, hoping for a glimpse inside. Now I felt as though I'd always been here. There was a lot of work to keep me busy and a lot of new people to meet—people from town I wouldn't otherwise have rubbed shoulders with. A variety of people lived in this small town in the Copper River Basin, and as the hub for the area, several small communities came to Glennallen, which had the amenities of a school, a post office, gas stations and a store.

Sally's familiar face came in from the entryway, and as the door opened, the snow blew in. Oh no, not a blizzard! I waved to my new friend and rose from my desk. I tidied my space, pumped some hand lotion on my hands, and grabbed my purse.

"Hi, Sally!" I'd met her at church, and she came in and did the evening cleaning at the hospital. "How were the roads?"

Sally brushed at her coat as she hung it on a peg near the door. "The wind just started to blow, so there weren't any drifts yet. I'd suggest you head home soon."

My coat was near hers, and I pulled it on, zipping it all the way up. "Thanks. I'd better get going then. I still need to go get the kids from school. I'll see you Sunday!"

I stepped out, and my face was blasted with icy-cold snowflakes. I could hardly see the buildings across the road.

Oh LORD, please help this drive be OK.

So far, Roy had been the one doing all the driving. With him on his mission trip, I'd be driving myself and the kids out to our cabin. Even before we'd moved to Alaska, I wasn't keen on winter drives. Now the responsibility was mine. I felt my chest tighten. Was it from the cool air?

The truck started without any issues, and I took the back roads to the school. As I drove up the steep road to the entrance, I accelerated to climb the hill. The back end of the truck fishtailed, and I eased off the gas. My heart beat wildly.

Dear God. It can't be like this. I need to get the kids and find our way home.

The truck responded to the speed decrease and climbed to the top of the incline. I eased into the parking lot, then looked to see the kids already bundled and outside waiting for me.

Rusty opened the door for Pam, and as they piled in, the truck filled with her excited chatter.

"Mommy, we learned about glaciers today, and I told my teacher I saw one this summer, and we saw a bear and an ocean and—"

Rusty cut her off before she could finish. "We know Pam. We were there, too." He let out a sigh. "Hi, Mom."

"Hey. Buckle up. It's snowing hard, and we need to head home. We'll have to do our grocery shopping another day. We need to beat the storm."

"Beat the storm? Mommy, you can't do that!"

"Just let her drive Pam. Yes, she can."

"Nuh, uh. Today, teacher told us glaciers are strong, and they push dirt and rocks and—"

"Pam, I only mean we need to go home before the roads get any worse," I said.

I gripped the wheel and moved across the parking lot, scanning the dark sky that loomed ahead of us. These short days didn't help. Thank God the snow was white and reflected any amount of light from the headlights.

"Why don't you think of a song from Sunday school that we can sing together?" I said. "I love hearing you sing."

"Oh, great," Rusty moaned. "Can I plug my ears?"

"Play along, Rusty. I need your help with your dad gone. Remember how he said you're the man while he's gone?"

My reminder must have encouraged him, as he made song suggestions and led Pam in hand motions, which helped pass time while we traveled out of town toward our cabin.

With each mile, the visibility decreased. The snow blew in from the north across our lane and formed drifts near the road's edge.

Lord, help me to see.

As the prayer went up, I saw a dark shadow come onto the road ahead.

"Hold on!" I pumped the brakes, and as we neared the form, I could see it was a large moose crossing the road. "A moose!"

Pam let out a scream as the truck fishtailed with my sudden braking. Thankfully, I didn't lose control, and we decelerated and straightened.

"I'm so glad that wasn't on a hill." I held the wheel and felt my arms ache from the tension I held within in my body.

Not only was there darkness this time of day, but this particular afternoon, there was snow blowing, and now, I was reminded that there also large animals to be cautious of. I was so glad this drive wasn't one I normally had to do alone.

"Look for a road sign," I said. "I can't remember how much farther."

We'd only been living out at our property for a few weeks. I hadn't memorized each turn yet, and with Roy driving most of the time, I hadn't had to depend on my recall. I hoped it wasn't more than ten miles to our cabin on the lake. Wasn't there one more long hill down? Then a sweeping curve to the right before the bridge? Not that I could see much more than twenty feet ahead of the truck.

"I see a mile marker, Mommy!" Not usually wanting to hear Pam's extra-loud voice, I was thrilled to have her help us and watch where I couldn't. I didn't want to peel my eyes from the road.

"What number is it, cubby?"

"It says…"

She must be searching to see.

"One, four, five."

"Oh good!"

Not much farther then. We were less than ten miles from home.

"Thank you, God. Please keep any other animals off the road." I prayed out loud. The kids needed to hear me call out to God for help.

We continued the rest of the way in silence. I scanned those last miles like I was searching for a treasure. At last, our driveway came into view.

"Yah!" Mommy, you did it!"

"Good land, I hope we don't have to do *that* again any time soon." I turned in, and when I saw the cabin, a wave of relief flooded over me.

Safe at home. Now it was time to tackle the evening chores. Thank goodness the kids were on Christmas vacation now, and we could hunker in. Was I ready for this lifestyle?

❄

"MOMMY, I GOT A CARD FROM HEATHER!" PAM WAVED A colorful paper, and Boo jumped to snag it.

I plucked off my boots and set them near the woodstove. The short walk to the mailbox on the side of the highway had chilled my feet. My boots needed a little more heat before I hauled more wood.

She ripped open another envelope, and pictures fell out from inside as she scrambled to grab them before the dog did.

"Whoa, be careful." I reached for the card and saw familiar handwriting.

With each Christmas card we received in the mail, I fell deeper into my homesickness for the only place I'd ever called home. I decided looking at cards could wait since I might tear up and I didn't want the kids to see.

"Mommy, was this your last day of work?"

"Yes, I explained on the way home, we all have a break now." I shivered from the cool air, which lingered in the cabin. After being gone all day, the fire was out, and I needed to start supper.

"Where will we have our showers if we don't have them at school?"

"Rusty, I don't know. Can you grab more wood from the porch? Sheesh it's cold in here."

I studied our cabin. *Which way should I go first?* I wished I didn't have to do all this extra work for simple things.

Pam swung her legs as she sat on the stool. "Mommy, can Betsie come over on break?"

She'd recovered from her fever a couple of days ago and was full of chatter this evening.

"No." I hoped she would hear the exacerbation in my voice. "It would mean we'd have to drive to pick her up, then drive to take her home. It could take hours."

"Yah!"

She didn't get it. I would not do all that driving on winter roads myself with Roy out of town on his trip.

"Probably not."

"Can I go to her place, then?" She jumped off the stool and held the door for Rusty, who brought in an armload of wood.

Was there a way to ignore her question? "It's the same both ways. Why don't you draw a picture for Heather?"

"I'll draw her a picture of the bear cubs I saw." Pam slammed the door behind her and ran to the bin of crayons.

Rusty rolled his eyes behind her back and stacked the wood by the stove. "Like the ones way back in the summer? I'm sure you already told her about them. Think of something else already."

"No, I just saw them!" Her little tongue stuck out, and I reached to give it a flick.

"Keep your tongue in your mouth there, little lady. And don't be making up stories for a Christmas card."

"I'm not."

I watched her and examined her face for signs of a lie. Why would she make this up? For attention, maybe?

"OK then, where?" Rusty came to her side, stood close and peered at her like he was ready to pounce on her answer.

"Over by the shacks." Her proud statement came with her nose in the air.

I moved to the woodstove with the propane torch to get the fire started and listened closely to the banter.

"That's impossible. The bears are sleeping now, Pam. In case you haven't noticed, it's winter."

"I'm not a dummy. I saw two bear cubs!" Her boisterous voice pricked my ears.

I turned the torch on and let it heat the coals from the bottom of the stove. "Draw a picture for me."

Whatever! What could it hurt? It hit me then, as I noticed the first spark ignite the log...heat! Maybe she was delirious when she was in her fever stupor and imagined the bears? I'd play along.

"What color were they?"

Rusty huffed and climbed the ladder.

"They were black, like my stuffy!"

The fire started to crackle and smoke. I pulled the door closed, leaving it open slightly so it would draft.

"Alright, Pam. I'll look at your picture when it's done."

"Thanks, Mommy!"

I picked up the cast-iron kettle, which I kept on the stove, and carried it to the water jug to pour more in. The steam helped put moisture into the air with the dry heat caused by burning wood.

Pam's voice grew high-pitched. "Where do you think the cubs' mommy is? It makes me sad for them to be alone."

"I don't know." This was becoming quite the story. I was sure her wild imagination would create an amazing tale of two cubs deserted during the winter! Probably starving, too!

I closed the woodstove door and held my hands over the top. It would be a while before it radiated heat. Now for supper? No need for anything fancy, it was just the kids and me.

"How about grilled cheese for supper?"

"Oh, Mommy, I love grilled cheese!" said Pam. "Do you think it will help my sore throat?"

The two cast-iron pans hung on a nail, and I leaned over to pull one off carefully, then placed it on the stove and dropped some oil in it. This system of cooking with one or two pans made for easy cleanup at the end of a tiring day.

"You have a sore throat?" I looked at the aggressive coloring she was doing with the crayons. "Not so hard you'll break them!"

"It hurts when I swallow, but grilled cheese will be good."

"Okay."

I busied myself with making supper and prayed there wasn't anything more to her complaint.

As I found the ingredients for a quick supper, I had jumbled feelings about looking at the mail. I didn't want to taint this joyous season with my selfish thoughts of home, but the letters tempted me, to rip them open later in private.

FINALLY, WITH THE KIDS ASLEEP, THE CABIN WARM, and my stomach full of hot food, I sat down to look over the cards from earlier. A brightly-colored card from Roy's sister and family brought a smile to my face. They talked of their Christmas plans, and I could imagine the familiar routine of visiting from house to house. I set it down on the table. When would we visit them next? These few months since we left on vacation felt like years.

I dug around for the large envelope and touched the writing on the front. From Faith! I opened it. Had she sent pictures?

DEAR LOU,

Being married is glorious, and we are settling in at the parsonage that the church finished shortly before our wedding! I will send the baby announcement soon! Kidding, but not really! Maybe we will have a baby in the next year!

I'm sure, by now, you're dashing through the snow and laughing all the way! What a winter wonderland you have! Thanks for the postcard. I'm thrilled to read that you work at the best hospital in the world! It has to be with a name like FAITH!

Love to all of you, and big hugs! I hope you can come home for a visit soon!

LOVE FAITH (AND JIM TOO)

. . .

WHAT COULD I WRITE IN OUR CARDS? *WENT TO ALASKA this year...job at roadhouse was a bust. Moved to the middle of nowhere. Learned to shoot a gun. Live in an igloo!*

Humph, I needed to bust out of this slump!

I wrote the number five on a scrap piece of paper. I'd find five things I enjoyed about the year. Surely, a Christmas card would be full if I mentioned them all.

A rose-colored envelope grabbed my attention. How had I missed it earlier? I opened it and gasped when I saw the signature at the bottom of the card. Birgit!

I read through the note at a rapid pace, anxious to know she was alright. I only caught a word here and there. *Slow down, Lou.*

DEAR FAMILY!

I LOVE AND MISS YOU ALL. I'M SURE YOU KNOW ALL TOO WELL THAT I WAS saddened to see you go so abruptly from Miner's. Also, I don't blame you in the least. My uncle has hardened his heart, and I have broken with his company. Perhaps one day he'll apologize and explain the events that occurred at Miner's and bring me peace.

I relocated to Wrangell, Alaska, to stay with extended family until I can sort out the finances with Miner's. Here, I am able to find work and live safely with those who truly care for me.

I wrote Fred and asked for your address. Will you please write me back and tell me of your adventures? I was shocked to see that your mailing address was in Glennallen! It sounds like you'll have stories to share with me!

I look forward to hearing from you soon.

A very Merry Christmas to my dear family!

LOVE, BIRGIT

. . .

A WAVE OF RELIEF SWEPT OVER ME, AND I HELD MY hand to my chest. She was okay! I'd have to tell the kids in the morning. They'd be so happy to hear from her. Maybe they could make her a card?

A loud ring from the telephone startled me, and my pen shot into the air. I grabbed the receiver.

"Hello?"

"Hi, Lou!" Roy's voice muffled through the line.

"Wow, I didn't think I'd hear from you!" I grinned.

He'd found a way for a call!

"There's a phone here at the school. How's everything there? Is Pam feeling better?"

I looked behind me. "She's good. We miss you!"

"I miss you too. We'll fly home tomorrow, but Fred says we'll need an extra day in town before we go to Glennallen. I wanted you to know so you wouldn't worry. If you need anything, call ahead a grocery list to the mission office in Palmer. I've got to go. Love you."

"Love you too. Thanks for the call."

I set the phone back. We'd come so far this year in our marriage. That wasn't something I could put in a Christmas card, but it certainly was an answer to prayer that I'd note in my prayer journal—Roy's care for us and his driving desire to be home. Did my attitude tarnish the shine I longed to burst through?

A thump up the stairs rattled the ladder to the loft, and I hurried to see if the dog was rapping at it to go up with the kids. Pam's legs dangled from above.

"Pam! Be careful. Are you coming down?"

I shot a brisk look at the clock. Nine? Why would she be up?

"There's a bumble bee jumping up here on my blanket."

I tapped her still-hanging foot. "Move to the ladder."

"Hey, it's going to fly to the marshmallow, so it's OK now."

"Pam, put your foot on the ladder!" I tugged harder and placed her foot on the rung.

Good land, was she sick again, or dreaming? I decided it was pointless to pull, so I climbed up instead and gave her foot a push. She pulled it back.

Once my head poked up, I saw her crawl to her bed. She put her feet up on the wall and her hands behind her head. I followed and felt her forehead.

"Tickle, tickle." She waved at me.

"I'm not tickling you." Her forehead seemed normal, so I figured she was dreaming. "Good night. Stay up here!"

As I climbed down, I remembered the nights alone when I tended to the kids before Roy and I were saved. Those days were long gone now, and I didn't want it to be the norm ever again.

Thank YOU, Lord for reminding me there's lots to give thanks for.

Before he left, Roy had instructed me on everything I needed to check while he was gone. I mentally reviewed the list and looked around the cabin.

I scooped up Boo and snuggled him in close before going to bed. We were well cared for!

Chapter 23

FACE TO FACE

"TAKE THEM OFF ME!"

Pam's emphatic cry in the middle of the night drove me from my bed and up the ladder to the loft.

"Hurry! Mommy! It's a big whale, and he keeps swimming in my pillow."

What was going on?

I turned the light on, and she shielded her face. She was curled up in a ball at the foot of her bed. "Can you help? Can you help?"

Her body rocked back and forth.

I felt the heat coming from her before I even touched her head. "Come to me." I rubbed her back.

Dear Lord, not again. Not with Roy gone!

Rusty sat up. "She's been at it all night. I'm going downstairs to get a drink."

"Pam, shh."

Her sweaty pajamas clung to my hand. I tried to fan her with the shirt she wore.

"It's the whale, Mommy." She blinked, and her gaze froze on me.

Something deep within me prompted me to play along. "He's swimming away. Yup, there he goes. You're OK, honey."

"Mmm, he's going?"

I put a fresh shirt on her and helped her change the rest of her clothes. I felt her bed. It was soaked. *Should she come downstairs with me? How can I get her down safely?* I stripped the sheets, laid her on the floor and gave her the stuffed bear cub, a favorite. "Cuddle with Cubby. I'll be back."

Lord, help me know how to help her!

I tossed the sheets in the kitchen corner and rushed to find dry ones. Anything to cover her bed. "Rusty, find some rags and a bowl of water. I need your help. Pam isn't fooling, she's sick again."

I opened the plastic bin Kim had given me and pulled out the fever reducing medicine.

Let it work fast!

My breaths increased, and I knew myself well enough to know I needed to stay calm to help my family. I recalled Kim's encouragement the last time Pam was sick, but after giving her the medicine, I'd call the clinic anyway. Was there a virus going around?

My movements were methodical. I dosed the medicine and helped her sip the liquid, careful not to spill it. Her moans rang in my ears. How does a parent take on their child's pain? I ached for her to be well. I stroked her head and looked at her fine features: her small hands and feet, her bony knees and elbows. This little package carried a punch! Was she so tenacious because of how hard she fought for her life the minute she was born? Would her delicateness be a constant reminder to hold her close?

I bathed her, and she sipped some water. Her eyelids were heavy. She slouched on me, and I eased her down to her bed.

Lord, help her rest!

I tiptoed down the ladder. Rusty sat on the couch, flipping through a magazine.

"She's asleep again if you want to go up. Careful to be quiet."

He gave me a hug and inched up the ladder. I gave him a thumbs up. I knew the hospital number by heart after working the front desk and hurried to dial.

"Hello, Faith Hospital."

A nurse was on duty day or night. It relieved me to hear a familiar voice.

"Kim, it's Lou. Pam has a fever again, and this time she is delirious. I just gave her a dose of the medication you gave me. Anything else?"

"I'm sorry to hear she's not doing well. It sounds like you are staying calm. Did you check her temperature?"

"I didn't. I was in a hurry to get her the meds, then she fell back asleep."

"It's OK. I'm glad she's resting. Lord willing, she'll sleep through the night and you can check her temperature in the morning. Look to keep her safe if she's agitated, and try not to argue with her; it may upset her more. Also reassure her that you're there, and maybe provide something familiar, like a favorite blanket or stuffed animal." Kim's advice was clear.

"Is there anything going around? A virus or flu?"

"There's always something making the rounds. You're doing a superb job. I've made a note of our phone call, and another nurse will call you in the morning to check on her and you." I sensed a reassuring smile over the phone.

"Thanks, Kim."

"Good night, Lou, and get some rest."

"Good night." I hung up the phone, ready to find my bed, knowing help was a phone call away if I needed it.

"Go ahead Rusty, take those to the mailbox. Later, if I get more done, I'll have you go again." I sent most of the Christmas cards with hopes they would arrive in time.

He yanked on the door. "I wonder why"—he yanked again—"the door is so stiff." It swung open with his last pull.

"I think it's warmer. Maybe there's some ice on the jamb. Thanks for taking those."

"Mommy?" Pam had slept all night and awoke feverish, but not as hot. She sipped some soup from a cup at the table.

"Yes." I wiped the table where she'd spilled and kneeled down next to her.

"Can I have some crackers?" She whined her question skillfully and looked right at me, her dark eyes pleading.

"Of course!"

I went to find a box, happy to give her whatever might add a bright spot to her day. Crackers and snacks were extras we didn't always have around, so they were considered a treat.

She dropped the blanket from around her shoulders. "First, I'll go to the bathroom."

"Put your coat on. It might be warmer, but it's still winter."

"All the water I drank!" She let out an exasperated sigh.

"All the water helps you get better! I'll have Daddy pick up some juice before he comes home."

"Yah, I love juice! Can it be apple?" I helped her put her boots on.

"Sure."

As I opened the door, I looked down the driveway for Rusty, who was already out of view. He was in a helpful mood, which made the time with Roy gone more tolerable.

I turned the radio on, curious to hear the aviation forecast for Roy's sake. I sat and waited to hear the report for Palmer airport where their landing was scheduled. *Would they be able to fly today?* What did he think of his trip? He wouldn't want to go again soon, would he? I hoped not.

My mental checklist of daily tasks took me to the jug of water to fill up the kettle on the stove. I passed the large picture window, and Pam stood watching me. She pointed to the woods behind the house and said something, her speech garbled by the pane between us. I motioned for her to come in. She didn't need to linger outside.

A few moments later, both kids stomped their way into the house, voices loud, talking over one another.

"I DID see them!"

"I'm telling you, Pam, you DIDN'T see them! Bears sleep in the winter. You must have seen something else. Go drink your soup or whatever it is. Maybe you need to go back to bed!"

His impatience clear, I intervened and stepped between them.

"Enough!"

He spun his finger by his head, mouthing *loco*. He went back to the couch and picked up a magazine he'd pored over before.

I stiffened, my face serious to stop the argument.

"Mommy, I saw the bears again."

I placed my arm on her shoulder. She was going too far. "Pam, we don't know what you are seeing, but there aren't any bears this time of year. Now stop making things up! Do you hear me?"

"But I saw the babies by the…"

"I said for you to stop. Here are your crackers." I wanted to throw them at the plate, but held them firm in my grasp and placed them on it instead. She was notorious for getting in the last word, and it was irritating. I felt her forehead, certain she was brewing a fever again since she was delirious about the bear cubs. The night before it was whales, and today it was cubs. I turned and rolled my eyes.

Oh, LORD, help me be patient.

"Oh no, I have to go again!" Pam dropped the cracker she'd picked up and ran for her boots. "It's emergency style, Mom!"

"OK, hurry, then." I turned on the burner under the kettle. Maybe some tea would help me relax and think about how to spend the day waiting to hear from Roy.

"The door, Mommy! It's hard!" I raced to help her and yanked on it with both hands. Later, Rusty and I might need to fix it.

She yelled out to me. "Fast as I can, Mommy!"

I leaned against the door as it shut. I hoped she would make it in time, because I didn't want to haul water and heat enough to bathe her in the house, nor did I want to drive to a neighbor's so she could shower—if she was sick. A working indoor bathroom this summer was a must!

Summer? Did I imagine myself here into the following year? Was it becoming home?

I plopped myself into a chair and heard Rusty counting behind me. "What are you up to?"

"Oh, counting the brow tines on this moose. This picture is amazing!"

He'd found creative ways to learn about hunting and trapping. He was well-suited for Alaska.

"Think of it, Mom, one day a moose walks right in front of the house." He walked over to the window, pretending his gun was in hand. "It gets closer and closer than—Mom! No!" He pushed close to the window.

"No?" I looked at him. What was his deal?

"Pam, the bears—MOM!"

I sprang from my seat. Pam was by the outdoor shed, kneeling and reaching forward as she inched closer to the black bear cub close to the edge of the tree line!

"Grab the gun, Mom, the momma bear must be close!" He tapped rapidly on the glass, and I prayed it would grab her attention.

Without time to grab a coat, I opened the door.

"*Pam!*" My throat hoarse from the dry air, I tried to yell louder and grabbed my boots. I shoved them on without looking.

Oh, Lord, help!

I scrambled out, feeling like I moved in slow motion. Would I get to her in time? I turned the corner of the house and saw her in plain view, closer to the lake. She stepped closer to the cubs.

"Pam, NO!"

She looked at me, then back at the cubs. She wasn't taking me seriously! The looming danger of a protective momma bear rang in my mind. "Pam, come!"

I stepped off the porch to grab my stubborn girl. A flash of black grabbed my attention. A large sow approached from the tree line to the right.

"God, no!" I raced to the door, fumbling at the frame to catch myself.

"Rusty, the gun!" Already breathless, I panted out the words again. "The gun!"

There he stood on a chair with it in his hands. He must have gone for it himself! I snatched it from him.

"Ammo?"

"Dad left it loaded." He spurted his words and panted.

I kept the barrel pointed down and sprinted to the porch. As I stepped off, then raised the gun up at the sow, I saw Pam to the left, away from the enormous bear. She must have seen it because she screamed, piercing the air with the most sickening, fearful noise I'd ever heard.

"Run, Pam!"

"*God, help me! What do I do?*"

The sow's movement increased in speed. Her head lowered, she held Pam in her sight for an attack.

I levered the bolt action, pressed the safety, and looked in my sight, which bobbed up and down with my hurried breaths. I tried to follow the sow, who came fast. *I have to shoot!*

I have to!

My baby!

Would it hit?

Oh, God! Help!

I inhaled deeply and held my breath. My fingers gripped the gun. I squeezed the trigger. The gunshot's deafening blow jerked me, and I stumbled back. Had it gone off? I was numb to pain and noise. All I wanted was to save my little girl. The bear continued to run at Pam!

"NO!" "NO!"

Pam's little legs carried her as she flailed in the snow. I watched her struggle and hurled myself at her. She wasn't gaining enough speed. The sow might get to her.

Her slight frame fell into the snow. Her cries grew louder and louder.

I fumbled with the rifle in my hand, and the snow held me back from hurrying. I raised one leg up after another and trudged to her. The snow made it feel like I was forging my way through wet cement.

Almost! I was so close to her.

Oh, Lord, help her get up!

"PAM!" I fell onto her, shielding her with my body, and gasped for air, sucking in deep icy breaths.

LORD!

Her screams deafened me. I winced and looked up. Was the bear's attack on us imminent?

What?

There it lay in the snow, about ten feet from us, lifeless and still.

Oh, God, we're safe!

Thank God! Dear Jesus!

"Shh. Pam, shh. We're OK." My breathing hastened with the realization that the danger was over.

My chest tight from the frigid air, I lifted myself from her and grabbed her to me. I clung to her, enveloping her in my arms. Her stiffened body softened as her sobs quieted. I stroked her head.

Boo inched between us, whined, and licked at her face. Her giggle from the affection broke our embrace as she raised her arm to push away the puppy kisses.

"Mom?"

My muscles felt frozen as I tried to get up and help her stand.

"Mom?"

Rusty! I turned to see him, a flat gaze across his face as he rubbed his eyes.

"Mom, you shot the bear!"

"Yes, yes, I did." I panted and pushed on my thighs. I raised myself up, blinking slowly. "Thank God, I did."

At some point, I must have thrown the gun down. I gathered it from the snow, quickly checked the safety, and clutched it against my chest. "Rusty, come take the gun."

Boo ambled through the snow and yipped at Pam as though he was escorting her to the safety of the cabin. He stopped at Rusty's feet and turned back to us.

With the gun safely in Rusty's care, I picked up Pam. She straddled my body and clung to my neck with her tiny arms. Her face, cool from the icy snow, pressed against mine. Her tears wet my cheeks, and I let mine flow to mix with hers. Let them fall wherever they may—on the snow, our coats. I didn't care. We were safe!

Chapter 24

HOME AT LAST

WE MADE OUR WAY BACK INTO THE CABIN, MY HANDS quivering as I dialed the clinic.

A voice I didn't recognize answered. "Faith Hospital."

"Hello, it's Lou." I was sure they heard the waffle of my voice. "I need help. I don't know who else to call."

"Hi, it's Alice. Tell me what's going on."

Now I recalled Alice, who worked in billing. We'd sat together at the craft night after work.

"I...I shot a bear."

Pam's grip on my neck loosened, and I eased her down to the floor.

"Are you OK?" Her voice, high-pitched, sounded concerned.

"Yes, we are all OK. Roy's still out of town. I don't know what to do."

"About an hour ago, a trooper responded to a medical emergency in your area. I'll have dispatch notify him. He'll probably come instead of calling you. Do you need anything else?"

Relief flooded me. Thank God someone was close. "No,

thank you."

I hung up the phone and stared at Pam. She had stopped crying and cuddled with Boo on the couch. Rusty sat next to her and stared at them.

I stepped onto the stool to put the gun back, not knowing what else to do with it except remove it from plain sight.

In the kitchen, I warmed coffee on the stove and stared at the flame. I shot a bear? We could've died or been mauled. I put my hands to my face to hide the emotion that flooded over me like water over the Hardy Dam in Michigan.

A knock at the door sent my heart racing.

How could someone be here so soon? I peeked out the window above my sink and saw the familiar coloring of a state trooper's vehicle.

I opened the door to a tall man holding a Stetson in his hand.

"Ma'am, I'm Trooper Yanker with the Alaska State Troopers. Can I come in?"

"Yes." I pushed the word out, scared of a reprimand in front of the children. I purposely broke eye contact with him and looked at the kids, who both held Boo back from leaving the couch.

"Is my Mommy going to jail?" Pam tucked her head behind Rusty.

"No, she's not." The trooper's smile filled his face, and he waved to the kids. He held their curious looks, not appearing upset. "Can you tell me more about what happened today?"

Pam stood up and gazed down. "I...I didn't do as I was told." Her eyes darted up and back "I had to go bathroom and saw the cubs." She shuffled her feet and stuffed her hands in her pockets. "I disobeyed Mommy when she said come. The Momma bear came after me. I wasn't hurting her babies."

I opened my mouth to explain, but Rusty started in. "My mom shot the bear. I thought it still was gonna get her, but it died before it got to where my mom laid on top of Pam." He puffed out his chest. "It took her one bullet to kill it."

"Hmm, impressive!" The trooper inched forward to the table, set down his hat and pulled out a notebook. "I didn't catch your name?"

Did he need my name for the ticket he would write me?

"Lou Wendel."

He held out his hand. "Lou Wendel, let me be the first to congratulate you on a job well done!" He shook my hand firmly. "I'll take it from here and cage the cubs to transport them safely. I'll dispose of the sow, unless you have plans for it?"

"I don't want the bear." I cleared my dry throat. "I figured I was in trouble." I searched his eyes. Was there more?

"No, not at all. You've the right to protect life and property. I'd say your determination and work to calibrate yourself to handle the rifle surely paid off. You risked your life to save your children." He wrote in his notebook, then put it in his front pocket of his external carrier.

"What are your names?" He took his hat.

"Pam!"

First to offer a name, she came to me and put her arm around my waist. I touched her head and stroked her hair.

"Rusty."

"Your momma would make a good trooper!"

Rusty picked up Boo and came to where we all stood. "My mom?"

Trooper Yanker laughed and knelt down. "Yes, she ran to the danger when you needed her. Most people run away from danger."

"I assure you, it's not a job for me."

"Ma'am." He gently placed his arm on mine. "You do it every day. I have the utmost respect for you. Moms are the most amazing people. It's an important calling you have, raising these two kiddos. Keep up the excellent work!"

The tears I tried to hold back rolled down my face, and I wiped them with my hand. I rubbed my palms up and down my shoulders to help put heat back in my chilled body.

Boo let out a bark, and we all laughed. Rusty rubbed the dog's head vigorously.

"One shot, eh?" The trooper petted Boo.

"Yes, one shot." I didn't bother to tell him that there was only one other time I'd shot the rifle and that I'd blighted the shot.

"I'm impressed. If I take the sow, I'll retrieve the bullet and you can have it as a keepsake. For now, I'll round up the cubs. Kids, when I'm done, I'll let you know so you can get close and see them."

"Right on!" Rusty put Boo down and went for his coat on the hook.

My resilient kids bounded back after the trauma of the day. However, I still felt rattled with shock and disbelief.

"Stay in here while he works." I pulled Pam closer to me and knelt beside her. "How are you feeling?" I cupped her face in my hands and assessed her temperature.

"OK, Mommy. I feel bad those cubbies don't have a momma."

"Me too, honey."

"Can you call me that?"

I stood and walked to get my coffee. "Call you what?"

"Honey cub!"

"Oh, great!" Rusty wrestled with his coat and geared up for going outside. "Honey cub, really?"

"Come have some water, honey cub. We need you to feel better." I poured her a tall glass and knew she'd drink about half. "Later we can make some Christmas treats for when Daddy comes home."

Rusty opened the door and shut it again. "He's loading them now." A big grin spread across his face. "I wonder why a bear family is out now, at this time of year? I sure didn't believe Honey Cub for one second."

A knock sounded at the door, and Rusty quickly opened it. He let the trooper in.

"Huh, those cubs are wet! I bet the den flooded, and it aroused them from hibernation."

"Flooded?" Rusty looked up at the trooper.

"There's a lot of overflow in the creeks 'round here. Want to take a picture with them before I go?"

"Yes!" the kids shouted in unison.

Boo barked and ran to the trooper.

"Ma'am?" He held my gaze and waited for my answer.

"Go ahead. Bundle up though!" I put my hands in my sweatshirt pocket.

Once Pam was ready, their excited voices followed the officer out the door.

A picture with the black bear cubs—no, thank you.

I COULD FEEL THE RUMBLE OF A VEHICLE DOWN THE driveway. The screech of brakes set my nerves on edge and gave me a chill up my back. I dropped my crocheting on the couch and raced to the door. Who was here? I locked the door and went to the window, ready to grab the phone if I needed help.

"Roy!"

His truck door was wide open, and he came around the front of the house.

"Lou, Rusty, Pam?" His shout echoed.

"Why is Daddy yelling?"

Boo barked incessantly as we scrambled to go out to Roy.

"Daddy's home!" Pam scrambled to the door as I unlatched it.

"Roy!"

He stood with his mouth open and ran to us.

"You're OK!" He whisked me up into his arms and grabbed me with a fierce hug.

"Daddy, Daddy!" Pam clung to his legs.

He set me down and gripped my shoulder. "What happened? There's blood at the end of the driveway, and then more here close to the house."

I clasped his forearms. "You're early!"

"Lou?" His gray eyes searched mine. He was breathing fast.

"You're a day early?" I blinked rapidly, trying to absorb his presence. "I'm so glad you are home! Can...can...we talk inside?"

The warm air from the house wafted out and created a misty cloud of condensation.

"Yes, if I can walk with this glob of goo stuck to my leg."

Pam giggled as she clung to Roy's calf.

Rusty stood in the doorway and threw his arms at him. "Dad!"

"Son!" Roy took him into his embrace.

We all stood on the threshold, wrapped in each other. I looked heavenward and closed my eyes.

Thank you, Lord. He's home safe. We are together.

"OK, let's get inside. I sense there's a story here, but it will be better with a cup of coffee in my hand on the couch."

"Oh, Daddy!"

We all helped him put up his winter gear. I busied myself making fresh coffee, and the kids explained our turbulent day. From the counter, I turned and watched the kids engage with Roy. I wanted to be alone with him and to be held. I licked my dry lips and took a sip of my lukewarm coffee. As I heard the story unfold, I felt the sting of tears form in my eyes.

I handed him his mug and sat across from him. His tender gaze at each of us spoke of his love and care. My jumbled mind hadn't had time to process the events yet. Still so raw from the chaos, I let myself sink into the couch and listen. I bit at my lips when the kids drew closer to the crux of the attack. Somehow, it all sounded so awful told back from their perspective. I couldn't hold back the tears, which flowed down my face.

"Come here." Roy held out his hand.

I went to sit next to him and rested my head on his shoulder.

"So, my very own Annie Oakley narrowed a shot to kill a bear. That's one amazing Alaskan momma!"

I bowed my head and placed my palm to my heart.

"God, You are faithful. You did this! Thank you!"

"Oh, Daddy, I was so sick! I saw elephants and whales and zebras and kangaroos—"

"You did not!" Rusty interrupted Pam and gave her a shove.

Roy's quizzing look spread across his entire face, and he cupped Pam's face in his hands. "How are you doing now, peanut? You look good to me!"

Pam's little sigh clued us in, and she savored it all. "I'm OK, but I'll do better after I have a snack." She gave me a side glance. "And maybe some juice."

"I don't think my heart has stopped pounding! Maybe a snack and some juice will be the cure. You'll have to get them from the truck since your daddy is the grocery-delivery man."

The kids raced to the truck. With the shut of the door, Roy came to me, wrapped his arms around me, and held me tight. I felt him breathe in deep, then let it out slowly. "I'm so proud of you, and so glad everyone is OK." He brushed at the hair on my forehead and looked at me, inches away from my face. I flushed from his close hug.

"I still can't believe it! God did it! You know how little I've shot a gun."

"I know you are one fantastic woman who let God help her become calibrated for his work here in Alaska." He chuckled and sipped his coffee. "It is your Alaskan Calibration!"

Chapter 25

ALASKAN

"SOURDOUGH? UGH, THAT SOUNDS HORRIBLE. WHY would someone call it sourdough? Do I have to eat it?" Pam scrunched up her nose at me as I ladled the mix onto the griddle.

Kim had brought over the starter the night before on her way home from work to check on Pam. The batter sizzled, and the smell of the hotcakes made my stomach growl with a fierce hunger. After the turbulence of yesterday, and Roy's surprise premature return, my body was on heightened alert, and I'd barely eaten.

"Come here, peanut!"

Roy scooped Pam up in his arms, swung her around and threw her on the couch. Her laugh filled the cabin. She was so loud I feared it might raise the roof!

"Let your mom finish cooking because I'm as hungry as a bear!" He roared and tickled her, only escalating her squeals.

"A couple of more flapjacks and breakfast will be done. Rusty, will you set the table please?"

He went to the cupboard and pulled out plates. "Mom, why do they call it sourdough?"

"The flour and yeast stay out at room temperature and the dough sours. After you take a scoop out, you add more flour and water. You can keep the mixture going for years. Folks here have kept sourdough going for ages. It's something they have when there isn't refrigeration. I don't know—it's worth a try." I whispered in his ear. "If you put enough syrup on, it'll be great!"

Our cabin felt so welcoming during breakfast, maybe because I wasn't the one feeding the fire, hauling the water, or checking off the to-do list. It was so good to have Roy home! We'd visited late into the night. I listened to him talk about his trip up north, and he asked me questions about the time he was gone.

"Alright, let's sit down." I removed the last of the pancakes and set them on a plate.

The fresh eggs from the neighbor, along with some frozen blueberries from the village Roy had visited, made our meal a truly Alaskan breakfast.

"Do you know what a sourdough is?" Roy grinned at the kids.

"Yah, Daddy. It's a pancake." Her smug look didn't seem impressed.

"Rusty, how about you?"

"Nope, I don't."

"Well, here in Alaska, they call someone who has spent one winter in Alaska a sourdough! We're halfway there! Huh, it's just occurred to me, that's what Birgit called me the first time we met and we had that flat tire."

It all came rushing back to me. I'd forgotten all about the note from Birgit. "I'm so sorry. I forgot to tell you we had a letter from Birgit!" I jumped up and searched through some paperwork for the letter.

"Really? Is she OK, Mommy?"

"Here it is. I'll read it."

I read the words slowly and watched everyone's faces brighten at the news that Birgit was safe with family and friends. We'd all grown to love her. At least now we knew she was OK.

"I don't want to be a sourdough, it sounds grumpy."

"Well, you ARE grumpy, and you have a sour face!" Rusty poked at Pam with his elbow.

She moved around to sit higher in her chair on her knees. "I think it should have a different name, like cookie dough! Sugar cookie dough!"

"Are you kidding me? I'm not calling you honey cub, and I'm not calling you sugar cookie dough!" Rusty rolled his eyes.

"Grab the hand next to you; let's pray." Roy looked at each of our faces and a smile spread across his. "Heavenly Father, thank You for Your Son, Jesus, and all He sacrificed for us. We're grateful for this time of year, when we focus on how You came as a baby and how You died to save us from our sins. Help us as a family to grow together, learning more about You and Your Word. We look forward to what You have for us here in Alaska. We're grateful for Birgit and her friendship and that she took the time to write. Help her to know what You have for her. Thank You for our family and for Lou preparing the delicious sourdough flapjacks. Amen."

Roy flopped some pancakes on his plate, then passed the plate, giving Pam a couple along the way. "I have an announcement this morning."

"We aren't moving, are we?" Rusty froze with the plate in his hand.

"Nope. While on my trip, I prayed constantly about whether the Lord is calling me into full-time ministry or not. I flew around with Fred and thought about being a pilot like him. The trip went well. I want you kids to know that God has impressed on me to minister full time."

He studied each of us one at a time, lingering on each face. He gave me a wink.

Early that morning, while still in bed not wanting to get out of the warm covers, we'd talked about his trip. I was so glad he'd shared this with me already, or I'd have been on the edge of my seat like the kids. While he was gone, I'd examined the last few months in my mind. Where was our family's destination? Was there another adventure? Would we stay, or move on? If he was called to serve full time, how would I fit in?

"I will be in full-time ministry with Lou." He pointed at me. "Rusty." He set his arm on his shoulder. Then he pulled at Pam's shirt. "And Pam. I mean, Sugar Cookie."

She clapped. "Daddy, that's my idea! I told you already! You ARE a missionary!"

"Yes, I am. And I have peace." He nodded his head at me.

I'm so glad we agree about this decision. I held my head up high.

Thank you, God! You always direct us.

"After coming home and hearing how your mom can fend off an army without me..." He winked at me.

I smiled at him, flushing at his compliment.

"I know my greatest mission field is here at home alongside your mom, raising the two of you. After school, I'm going to look around town for a job. We'll never know what life might throw at us, but we'll do it as a family."

AT THE EDGE OF THE LAKE, THE BONFIRE CRACKLED, and the flames leaped to the sky. I pulled off my mitts and held my hands close. The warmth of the fire on the chilly New Year's Day warmed my arms, shoulders, and legs. I turned my face away, lessening the heat on my cheeks and forehead.

"Mommy!" Pam threw herself at me and squeezed my legs tight.

"My little sugar cookie!" I kneeled to give her a hug and embraced her, savoring the affection.

"I'm so excited to see my friends!" She threw her hands in the air, hopped on one foot away from me, then fell back into a snowdrift and made a snow angel.

"They should be here any minute." I looked up at the blue sky and scanned the treetops.

"Lou, can you give me a hand?" Roy carried a small card table. Normally an easy task, but cumbersome through the snow, he held it up high.

Rusty came out of the cabin. "I got it!"

I waved at him in thanks. Flushed from the fire, I felt myself melt at the memory of the past week. The visit from Fred and Judy and then another week off work. It was such a sweet beginning for a new year.

The boys set up the table near the fire and brushed it off with their gloves. Roy's idea of company seemed cumbersome at first. Where would everyone sleep? Just like always, though, he found a way to make it happen with a nearby cabin the neighbors used for guests.

"Shh, listen." Roy put his hand to his mouth. "I hear an engine."

I looked up to the sky, and just above the trees, an airplane came into view. The hum of the engine grew louder and then zoomed over our heads.

"Yah, they are here!" Pam bounced around the bonfire in a circle.

The plane looped and circled the lake. It slowly descended on the ice and pulled in close to where we stood. The prop slowed, and the engine died. A door opened and out came Judy running at me!

"Lou!"

I hurried to meet her and held her tight. "I'm so glad you could come!"

"Are you kidding! I could hardly wait! You think the kids are excited! I paced the floor all morning! I want to hear it all!"

Cheerful voices danced on the ice, and the crunching snow sparkled under their feet. I didn't know if I could describe the uniqueness of winter in Alaska to friends back in Michigan. The colors, textures, and experiences were unlike anything I'd ever known.

"I guess I'm just the pilot!" Fred waved from the plane. He walked to us, his arms full of bags. "Kids! Come and grab a few things."

"Oh, here, let me help." Judy reached to lessen the load and handed me a box. "Here, it's for you!"

I looked into her bright eyes. A wide smile crossed her face.

"Thanks," I said.

I pulled my mitts off and set them on the card table along with the box. I pulled at the flaps and took out the yellow tissue.

"I know you like that color." Judy clasped her hands in front of her. She beamed.

I unfolded the tissue, which revealed a recipe book.

"Bear Tails and other Delicacies" I laughed, opened the cover, and flipped through the pages of the hard-bound recipe book. "I suppose this will come in handy one day!"

"More of a joke, but some of them look tasty! There's more. Keep digging."

A jar of canned salmon sat at the bottom.

"Wow, what a treat!"

"I hope you like it. It's fully cooked, simply open it and make a sandwich or fry it on the stove for salmon patties. You'll do just fine. I have more in the plane for you."

The last item I pulled out was a Christmas tree decoration. I held it up to the light. The hard texture felt like clay. "Did you make it?"

"Yes, just for you!"

Beautifully polished, the ornament sparkled in the low light of the day.

"What is it, Mommy?" Pam came close and reached for the ribbon.

"The Alaska flag!"

Judy pointed. "Look closely at it. There's a deep-blue background, and yellow stars that form the Big Dipper."

I rubbed my hand along the smooth front.

"Thank you, Judy, it's beautiful."

"My teacher said the Alaska muddo is..." Pam twirled in place. "Um it's..."

I laughed and Judy finished her sentence for her, thankfully. "The Alaska motto?"

"Yah, that's it! She said it is 'north to the future.' Does it mean I have to live here forever?"

Pam didn't wait for the answer and zipped away as quickly as she'd come. Thank goodness she was feeling better! Much better.

Fred placed a hand on my shoulder. "You've arrived!"

I laughed and shook my head. "No, I haven't."

"Oh, but you have! The last star in the bottom of the constellation points to Polaris—the North Star. You've found your way to and in Alaska. You're making it your home."

Could I have dreamed my longing for an adventure at fourteen would bring me on my long journey to where I stood?

I looked to Roy, and he grabbed my hand.

"It's true, we're home. I feel it." I leaned my head against Roy's shoulder and watched the laughing kids play on the lake. The cool air nipped my nose, and the frost formed with each of my breaths. The smoke rose from the wood stack. Our rustic cabin on the edge of the lake was only part of what made this our new home. Our hearts were at home and at peace with where God had led us, too.

Thank you, LORD, for bringing me home to Alaska. You knew I didn't want to come, but I'm so glad I did!

THE END

EPILOGUE

DECEMBER 24TH, 2020

I SET ROY'S TRAVEL MUG UNDER THE HOT WATER FROM the tap and filled it. As usual, I preheated his cup for the piping coffee I was about to add. I peeked out the window and saw the level of snow on the railing outside. Another inch had fallen the night before, maybe more. Then I looked to the thermometer close to my calendar that displayed both the inside and outside readings. Ten above zero. Thankfully, it wasn't too cold for our trip today!

Our home was cozy and warm. Would it be OK to leave for a few days to see Rusty, Julie, and the kids? For the last several years, our winters had been spent out of state in sunny Southern Utah near Jim and Faith. The church they'd started after moving from Michigan to Utah had grown over the last thirty-five years, and now we considered it our church—full of family and friends we loved to visit with over the winter months.

I tucked the pillows in at the couch. Roy's whistle carried from the other room. As I gazed out the large window looking out over the lake, I saw a familiar moose eating a willow. Ah, she was back nibbling again.

I loved living on the lake and all the wildlife we'd seen there over the years. We'd enjoyed watching this moose for a few weeks as she wandered around the lake's edge. Maybe next spring she'd have calves following her lead.

Yes, this had been a unique winter, with us staying in Alaska. Unable to travel because of COVID, we'd decided to stay, instead of driving out in our coach.

Pam and her crew were out of state now, so our visits with them weren't as frequent this winter as when she, Glenn, and their four kids had been in Anchorage.

Rusty was in Tok, so we'd seen him a number of times lately. He'd invited us for Christmas with some of their friends.

"Ready?" Roy walked down the hall from the bedroom and searched my eyes.

"Yes. I'll just fill your cup. My bags are by the door." I went to the kitchen, dumped out the hot water and replaced it with freshly made coffee from the coffee maker.

"How many years do you think it's been since we've been here at home for Christmas?"

It was a good question. The last time I remembered was when Rusty's oldest son had been about five.

"I think it's been about twelve years. Remember when Rick burned his hands on the woodstove. He wasn't used to it being hot because we are usually gone through the winter. The propane didn't work that year when it was time to cook." I smiled at him as he gave me a grin and raised his eyebrows. "The same year I gave away the tree decorations to the grandkids."

Roy went to the window and closed the blinds. "I remember."

We walked out, securing the doors behind us. Being out on the lake by ourselves meant risking someone snooping around and maybe forcing their way in to rob us. Times had certainly changed in the forty-plus years of living in our rural community. It wasn't as safe and secure as it had been. Each time we left, I'd say a silent prayer asking for God to protect our home. He'd been faithful, and we'd had no issues.

I rubbed my glove along the wide logs. We'd saved money for a number of years before moving out of the old cabin and into the log home that Roy and Rusty had built. Our house had endured the forces of wind, permafrost and earthquakes. It held so many memories of Pam and Rusty—and now our seven grandchildren. Would this be our last winter home now that we'd ventured south over the years? Yes, we'd need to fix a few things and maybe find something smaller with less maintenance. Was a chapter closing in our lives?

I shut the truck door and tucked a blanket around my legs. Some things never changed, and my need for warmth had only increased. "It's so good to get away, even if it's just for a few days."

"Tired of me, huh." Roy's tease didn't come as a surprise.

I'd found ways to tease him back. "I'm going with you, aren't I?"

The Ford truck we'd brought back up from Utah warmed fast compared to the diesel we'd usually driven in Alaska. Down our driveway a short distance, we came to Rusty's driveway.

He'd cleared the drive years ago with thoughts of building a house on the lake, utilizing several acres adjacent to our property. He'd even had the old cabin hauled over to his lot, hoping to fix it up one day. However, his job had taken him around to various parts of the state, and he'd never gotten around to it. I saw the moose nuggets on his drive and chuckled.

The light from the sun barely shone above the Chugach Mountain Range to the south. This time of year, it rose above the peaks before setting. I attached the auxiliary cord to the stereo when Roy got out to lock the gate to our driveway. Earlier

I'd downloaded the podcast from Jim Fales' Sunday sermon. While away, we kept up with Bible teaching, especially now since we'd been avoiding crowds. However, this week, we'd decided to set all that aside and enjoy visiting the folks at Faith Chapel along with Rusty and his family. I was still amazed at how Rusty's life took him full circle from starting out in Tok with us to raising his family there.

After Roy locked the gate, he hopped in. How did he manage to still move with ease at the age of eighty? He rubbed his hands together and looked over at me.

"Will you warm my hands up?" He shoved his hands near my blanket and held mine. "Aw, that's better. Did you bring my iPad?"

"Yup. Julie says she'll help me organize my pictures. We need to figure out how to un share all of yours."

Roy smiled. "What? You don't like all my pictures of cars and old, groovy trucks."

"Not really. I'd rather have pictures of the kids."

"I have lots of those, too."

"Did you text Rusty or Julie and let them know we're headed out?"

"Done."

He sipped his coffee and turned on his left blinker in preparation for turning to Glennallen. One hundred and seventy miles between our place and the kids.

Lord, please help us have a safe trip. Keep us on the road and the animals off.

My usual prayer was one we'd put into practice decades ago. Lord willing, we'd have an uneventful trip.

The truck gained speed as it headed east. We rode with silence between us and listened to the sermon. It finished just as we passed through Glennallen. I saw a few cars parked outside the clinic where I'd retired twenty-one years ago. "Roy, it seems a lifetime ago that I worked there."

"Lou, it has been. I've almost been retired as long as I worked for the state."

JUST AS I EXPECTED, ROY GOT HIS "USUAL" FROM Posty's along the way. Posty's was a small store on the Tok cutoff, where we enjoyed visiting with the owner and Roy would get a treat for the road. "How was your ice cream bar?" I asked.

"Delicious." He took the wrapper and placed it in a small garbage bag we had in the truck. Then he handed me a dime.

"What's this?"

"It's the change. I paid her with cash."

I clasped the dime and then tossed it lightly in the air. "Remind you of anything?"

"I've been thinking about that phone call I made years ago." He tipped his hat and smiled wide.

"Oh."

"Yup, I've been thinking if it was one of the wisest things I've done."

I pressed my lips together. "Um-hmm. And then you realized it led to the best thing that ever happened to you?"

"Right!"

I took my coat and reached to place it on the back seat when the truck began to slide out of control.

"Whoa." Roy steered with two hands. "Hold on, Lou."

I grabbed at my door.

Help us, God.

The truck fishtailed and the back swerved to the left, spinning us around into the snowbank where we came to sudden halt.

"Good land! You were saved on Christmas Eve. Were you trying to go to heaven on Christmas Eve?"

"I've never gone into the ditch in the winter before. Wow, that road is slick."

I shifted in my seat and looked around. We weren't in cell range, so my phone would do me no good. What now?

Roy reached for his gloves and turned the engine off. "Guess I'll try and get out and see what I can do."

As he put on his second glove, a car pulled in from the other direction and came to the edge of the road. A woman rolled down her window.

"It's icy! Can I make a phone call for you? You're going to need some help."

I recognized her voice but couldn't place where I'd met her before. Wow, she had a phone that worked!

Thank you, Lord!

I leaned over so my voice would carry past Roy. "Can you call my daughter-in-law? I'll give you her number."

The woman rolled her window down farther. "Here, I'll dial it then hold it out to you."

She put in Julie's number, and they spoke for a bit, then she held the phone out her window.

Roy shouted out to her, telling her our location. Sounded like she would come with the kids.

The good Samaritan drove off after we reassured her help was on the way.

Roy started the truck and turned up the heat. "Well, might as well get comfortable. It will be a bit. I don't know if I can even get out of my door. I doubt Julie will be able to pull us out with the Excursion. But at least this way, if she comes, we can catch a ride back and come back later when Rusty is off work or call a wrecker." Roy looked behind him and then down the road. "We're about forty miles from Tok."

I rubbed my hands together and took off my boots, tucking my feet underneath me and into the warmth of the blanket. "If this were our first date, I would have been thrilled to be stuck with you in the snow. But…"

Roy laughed. "It would've been great. However, I'd have been the laughingstock of town if I'd put my car in the ditch that day, and you might not have talked to me again."

"I'm sure I would've."

We'd hardly visited for more than a few minutes when a truck pulled in close, followed by a second vehicle. Roy rolled his window down again.

A man stepped out of his vehicle and waved. "Hey, Julie called and told me I'd find you here. My name is Darren. I only live a couple of miles down the road. I have some gravel I'll spread on the road then I think I can pull you out. My wife is in the other truck if your wife needs to get out and get warm." He glanced around our car. "Never mind, doesn't look like either of you can get out." He pulled his hat down around his ears. "Rusty is a friend. He said your grandson did some ditch diving earlier this winter. It's been an icy year."

"Thanks, we really appreciate it. I feel bad not doing anything."

The man waved his arm at Roy. "No worries." He went to the bed of his truck and opened the tailgate.

The man's wife walked over from her truck and helped him spread some gravel with a shovel, then he repositioned his truck. He came over with a tow strap and hooked onto our Ford.

Lord, I hope this works.

I didn't pay much attention to how much time passed as he did some shoveling around the truck and ahead where we'd need to drive out. We'd been helped by good Samaritans before. It was such a comfort to know they still existed.

The truck jerked as Rusty's friend gave it a yank, and out we came onto the highway.

Oh, thank goodness that worked!

"Lou, do you have some cash? I'm going to offer to pay him."

I dug in my purse and handed him some bills.

Roy stepped out and visited, offering to pay Rusty's friend. He refused the money and shook Roy's hand. "Happy to help. That's what it's all about up here. Keep your money and enjoy your Christmas."

Just as he walked back to his truck, Julie pulled up on the other side of the road. She rolled down her window. "Looks like we showed up just in time."

Roy walked over to her. "Sorry you had to come. I didn't know help was on the way."

"I got ahold of Rusty, and he reminded me to call Darren. Guess we'll see you back at the house. I'll follow you just in case you have any issues."

After telling Darren and his wife thanks again, Roy climbed back into the truck and we headed for Tok with Julie and the kids behind us.

"That was some added excitement for everyone." Roy sipped his coffee, and we sat in silence, our gazes fixed on the icy roads.

When we pulled into the driveway, Rusty had arrived home from work. He stood with his arms open wide, smiling.

We all stepped out of our vehicles and took turns with hugs. Safe with family. A Christmas together in Tok.

Thank you, God, for a safe trip!

WANT TO KNOW ABOUT LOU'S LIFE FIVE YEARS AFTER they've moved to Alaska? Want to join her on a moose hunt? I'd love to give you the short story Alaskan Harvest for signing up for my newsletter where you'll get exclusive deals, giveaways, and news. Grab your FREE copy and continue with the story today!

ACKNOWLEDGMENTS

An enormous thanks to my husband and kids for being patient with me while writing and editing this first novel. They've encouraged me, helped me think through scenes and outlines, and generated ideas. I love you all so much!

How many words can you use to describe big? Huge? Gigantic? I need as many words as I can to describe the massive help I've received from my writing peeps; Sara Blackard, Jody Basye and Shelly Sulfridge. I am truly grateful for your hours of help. Without this writing group I'd be left still thinking about writing instead of publishing.

AUTHOR

Alaskan based author Maryann Landers writes women's faith filled fiction based on true stories of extraordinary women of her magnificent state. She loves to showcase the unique north and give her readers a little taste of rustic Alaska.

While writing in her log home in the woods she is also planning her next adventure with her Alaskan husband, juggling mom tasks such as crafting homemade meals from moose and caribou meat, building DIY projects from a scrap wood pile and guiding her teens in their homeschooling.

To learn about her inspiration to write Alaskan based stories read her blog.

https://www.mary-ann-landers.com

Her first novel in the Alaskan Women of Caliber Series; Alaskan Calibration released June 2021.

ALSO BY MARYANN LANDERS

Book 2 of Alaskan Women of Caliber Series

Alaska Calling

Releasing in Fall of 2021

Made in the USA
Columbia, SC
29 June 2021